ZEBRA CROSSING

MEG VANDERMERWE

ONEWORLD

A Oneworld Book

First published in North America, Great Britain and
Australia by Oneworld Publications, 2014

Originally published in South Africa by Umuzi, an
imprint of Random House Stuik (Pty) Ltd, 2013

ISBN 978-1-78074-430-8
ISBN 978-1-78074-431-5 (eBook)

Printed and bound by Nørhaven A/S, Denmark

This is a work of fiction. While, as in all fiction, the literary
perceptions and insights are based on experience, all
names, characters, places and incidents either are products
of the author's imagination or are used fictitiously.

Oneworld Publications
10 Bloomsbury Street
London WC1B 3SR
England

ZEBRA CROSSING

Joy and gladness will be found there,
thanksgiving and the voice of song.
OLD TESTAMENT

We tell stories not to die of life.
ANTJIE KROG

For Sumarie: for your love without borders
For Selma Friedland (in blessed memory)

Prologue

'Tell me, learners, what is a border?'

For some, dawn is the loneliest time. But not for me. I rise with the living, the sun and the rock pigeons' chorus. I watch the light dress rooftops, car parks and, beyond them, the mountain. Then it comes: memory. You see, even after all that has happened to me, I still have my past for company. It creeps out of dark corners and gathers round like specks of slowly spinning dust. Familiar faces and places return. And those questions that still demand answers.

'Tell me, learners…'

Late 1990s. Primary school. Zimbabwe. I am seven. Our headmaster, Va Pfende, teaches us that Africa's borders were drawn many years ago. Va Pfende was a veteran of the war of independence in the 1970s and he likes everyone to know it. Using a bamboo stick, he points to the map of Africa that hangs on the classroom wall below a portrait of our President.

'It was the imperialist murungu,' *our headmaster explains, 'he came long ago, dividing this continent like the carcass of an ox,*

and kept the lion's share for himself. Remember, pupils, matsoti haagerane. *There is no honour among thieves. Thankfully, our great Zimbabwe is now independent. But never forget: once your parents and grandparents were slaves to greedy foreigners.'*

As the sunlight hits the shop windows, so that triangles of gold appear in their panes, I recall how obediently we scribbled down 'greedy foreigners', pledging to commit Va Pfende's words to heart in case Ian Smith and the other British colonialists, like locusts, ever threatened to return.

On that classroom map, national borders were drawn in purple. When my brother George and I reached the border at Musina, it was too dark to see whether those purple lines existed in real life. But since that September night, I have crossed that and other borders many times. Flown so high above them that below looked like an infant's patchwork puzzle. Flown so low that I could smell the dust and see the dry seeds waiting patiently for the rains to come and split them open. On those journeys I have seen that, in reality, no borderlines are tattooed across this earth. Forests and valleys, deserts and rivers, they know nothing of borders. Instead, they exist only in the minds of politicians, who guard their man-made borders with soldiers in uniform, wearing black boots and carrying clipboards and AK-47s.

'What is a border, learners?'

If I were in that classroom today, I would raise my hand and answer: a border is a place where barbed wire and high fences block your way.

It is where you are not wanted, but where you must nonetheless go.

It is where you must wait, terrified as you are, for the right moment to take your chance and dance with fate, while high above you in the starlit sky, the migrating swallows pass back and forth unhindered.

A border is where you must say goodbye. You cannot afford to turn and look back. The past is the past. That is what your brother says.

Borders rhymes with orders. You follow your brother's orders. You have no choice. Time to go forward, he says. To look forward.

A border is where you swap home for hope.

One

Four in the afternoon. George should be in the main house, squeezing a jug of mango juice or whatnot for our mistress. She will be where she is every afternoon after another beauty treatment at Mrs Mabeeni's parlour – in the sitting room, curled up on the leather sofa like a pampered pet, watching satellite television or flicking through *Cosmopolitan* magazine while eating Choice Assorted Biscuits. But instead he has come to see me in the outside courtyard, where I am wringing out the mop.

He knocks a cigarette from its pack and slips it between his lips. His face is sour. So, a dark mood. Another row with Mai Mavis, the cook? I know better than to ask. Must wait. Wait patiently until he decides to tell me. My brother sucks in, and then blows out.

'This time she has gone too far...'

I notice his hand is trembling.

'I won't protect her. I will confess to everything.'

Confess? He pulls on his cigarette. A cloud of smoke.

'I mean, did I not do only as she *told* me to? Should I now be punished for that bitch's stupidity?'

I listen. *Little sister*. I am seventeen. It is my job to listen. When I am not scrubbing, or sweeping. But most of all it is my job to obey. If I do not obey, how can he protect me?

The General's third wife is young enough to be his daughter. She and the General have been married for one year, ever since Mr General divorced Wife Number Two, and promoted this wife from being his 'small house' – his mistress. Wife Number Three has it all – youth, beauty and an education, but it is true that, since their marriage, the General's attentions have once again begun to wander. There is gossip among the servants. He is courting the flirtatious Miss Patience. He is interested in Miss Hazel, a woman with round, jiggling breasts and questionable morality.

But now, new developments, my brother says. So perturbed is he that he can hardly articulate his words. Wife Number Three has been caught red-handed in another man's bed. George swallows. She is in serious shit with the General.

'Before the day is through, he will interview all of us. He is certain she could not have managed it without the servants' help. We will be interrogated, then dismissed.'

My brother drops his cigarette stub and, his hand shaking, immediately lights another. Then he begins to pace. I know he colluded with our mistress. All the servants did. George often complained that they had no choice. They wanted to keep their jobs. But what now? *Hayiwa*? George looks desperate. The General is a rich and influential man in Beitbridge. He will see to it that my brother cannot find another job.

'And to make matters only worse,' George says, gesturing to me as though to a blocked toilet or some other annoyance, 'you know how they feel about peeled potatoes like yourself...'

Peeled potato. That is what many in Zimbabwe call me. Also

'monkey' and 'sope'. There are other names, too, depending where you go. Name rhymes with shame. In Malawi, they call us 'biri'. They whisper that we are linked to witchcraft. In Tanzania, we are 'animal' or 'ghost' or 'white medicine'. Their witch doctors will pay handsomely for our limbs. In the Democratic Republic of the Congo, they call us 'ndundu' – living dead. If a fisherman goes missing, they call on us to find the body. In Lesotho, we are 'leshane', meaning half-persons, whereas to South Africans, depending on whether they are Xhosa or coloured, we are 'inkawu', meaning ape, 'wit kaffir', 'spierwit' or 'wit Boer'. Meanwhile, my brother calls me 'Tortoise'. He says I always perform my tasks too slowly. Sometimes, though, I am 'Little Sister'. All the whites in these places simply call people like myself 'albino'. I also have a real name, though. My name is Chipo. In Shona it means 'gift'. When my mother gave it to me, I wonder, did she have a premonition about her daughter's destiny?

'Oh, to hell with them all,' George says finally. His mood has changed. Storm clouds are brewing in his head. He drops the stub of his second cigarette and twists it under his shoe.

'Put away that mop and gather your things. We're going home early, Tortoise.'

'In South Africa there are plenty of jobs,' George says. 'We won't have to crawl on our hands and knees to earn a pittance. And they have proper hospitals and shops *crammed* with cool goods like flatscreen TVs, and all the roads are clean, paved – not these bloody moon craters. That is because in South Africa…'

On the opposite pavement a woman is selling delicious, roasted sweet potatoes smelling of caramel. A few years ago those potatoes would have sold in moments. But money is tight for everyone these days, and what was once a small treat has become an unaffordable luxury for most. I watch her poke at them with a fork as George repeats the same promises about life over the border that he has been reciting to me daily since Mama passed away three years ago. I say nothing. My stomach grumbles from hunger and I pull my umbrella lower to protect my eyes. My spectacles have steamed up. It is too hot even to think. A stray dog trots past, one of those location specials, a little bit of every breed. Its tan-coloured ears and tail are pointing upwards, its red tongue is hanging out and its ribcage makes me think of prison bars. Sometimes these strays are hit by cars. Then their carcasses are left to rot at the roadside. Food for the rats.

I think of the General. Big cats like the General always catch rats like George and me. What will happen? George had to lie and tell the General that we have been called home because our mother is sick – so, an emergency. Otherwise we would not have gotten permission to leave.

'Bastard. Doesn't even remember we are orphans.'

We had to leave our week's wages as proof we would return for our interrogation about our mistress's lover. George spits. So now we are without a week's wages. And without jobs. What will tomorrow bring? Had George even thought of that?

If you had passed us in the street that afternoon, could you have known that once we both attended school, like the General's own teenage children, and had dreams and ambitions of our own? George wanted to start his own business. I secretly hoped one day, somehow, to qualify as a social worker or district nurse. What is more, our mother, when she was still alive, owned a brick house, which, although much smaller than the General's imposing home, had two bedrooms and an indoor bathroom with a flushing toilet. From that house our mother operated a lucrative drinking tavern called 'Old Trafford', named after her beloved Manchester United's home ground. There, surrounded by posters of David Beckham and Dwight Yorke, she served *mazondo*, boiled hooves and hard-boiled eggs, as well as a potent home-brewed beer called Seven Days, which caused her patrons to return faithfully time and time again.

A minibus taxi speeds past, its sides smeared with red dust, like chilli powder. Too full for us? Or maybe it is me they do not want to stop for. Two men pass. Too close. I can feel them staring. I look at the ground. My feet in my *zhing-zhong* flip-flops from the Chinaman shop are red from the dust, too. I must give my toes a good scrub tonight. Not that it matters. We can't keep the dust out of our house, though the place is never filthy – I make sure of that.

In 2003 the government declared informal drinking taverns like Mama's illegal. Operation 'Remove Moral Filth', they called it. The taverns encourage Zimbabweans to be sinful. That is what the government radio and newspapers shouted. All informal drinking taverns must be demolished. Street markets, too. If you don't do it, the police told us, then they will.

'What are you waiting for? Bring your hammers,' Mama said, standing in front of Old Trafford. Her skin quivered with rage. Maybe she was feeling very brave, or maybe she didn't believe they would dare to deliver on their bold promises. Either way, I think that if she could have killed that policeman at that moment, she would have. The head policeman had smiled and walked away.

Some say he had seen Mama at the rallies supporting the MDC. That is why she and Old Trafford in particular were targeted. Whatever the reason, one month later to the day we were woken by the rumble of their trucks.

Will we soon be in a truck? I wonder to myself. Jumping the border? Every day, they say, hundreds are doing it. That is what the radio and newspapers tell us. And then what? That truck will carry us from here to...? I look up in the direction of the border, over and beyond. From here to...? I cannot imagine what it looks like, in spite of George's stories. What does it look like? Johannesburg. Cape Town. They don't sound or rhyme like anything. Just names. I rub my eyes. They are burning from the heat and the dust. My umbrella is not helping much.

It is true that even before the demolition there were times when Mama admitted, 'I am not hungry, Chipo' or, 'Yo, I feel so, so tired! The tavern is wearing me out!' But there is no denying that, after it was destroyed, within eighteen months her health took a turn for the worse and so did our fortunes.

'Tortoise! Pay attention!' My brother sucks his teeth, irritated. 'Deaf as well as blind.'

I push up my glasses and lift my umbrella to squint at him.

'I said you better cook *sadza* for one extra tonight and buy a bottle of *chibuku*. I am going to invite Michael to join us. I need his advice about crossing the border.'

Michael is a distant relation of ours, and George's best friend. They have been best friends since primary-school days. Michael is a car mechanic who often boasts to my brother that he can repair a Toyota Land Cruiser with parts from a tractor. 'No one would even notice,' he says. When he was a boy, Michael and his father used to water down bottles of petrol with cooking oil and sell them at the roadside. They did this for three months before they were caught.

Michael works for a garage next to Mr General's taxi shop. It caters to the many trucks and minibuses passing back and forth, transporting people and goods between Zimbabwe and South Africa. He and George love car talk. But they can also debate for hours about Manchester United – which players are decent, worthy of wearing the red shirt, and who are 'buckets of shit'. Michael, I know, has no desire to go and 'try his luck' in South Africa. He is content where he is, he says. But his cousins, David and Peter, are already there.

David and Peter. Peter and David. Twins, though not identical. Peter can sing. David cannot. Peter likes Coke. David, Fanta Orange. I remember the first time I saw them at school. I was only six. And I can see them both standing in our yard waiting for George to finish his chores so he could play soccer. Once, Peter called me ugly: 'She looks like a monkey!' and David beat him. Then, in 1997, their father lost his job and they moved to Harare.

Another minibus is approaching. George sticks out his hand and it slows to a stop. The *hwindi* pulls back the sliding door.

'The General has done us a favour… You will see… We are going just in time. Next year the whole world will want to be in South Africa… The World Cup – that is the what. First time it is being played on African soil.'

The other passengers' eyes narrow and I choose a seat on my own, next to the window. George slumps down next to me and leans back against the torn seat cover. Soon the minibus is bumping over the potholed road. My buttocks will be black and blue long before we reach our home in Luthumba, I think, as George gives me a rare smile.

'I've heard that David Beckham will be there. Imagine that. I will definitely secure his autograph.'

An old man in a front seat wipes the sweat from his forehead with his sleeve. Another picks his nose.

'But not you, Tortoise. If he sees you, he would get such a fright he might run away.' My brother laughs and I can feel the other passengers staring again, so I say nothing.

Mama always said she was Zimbabwe's most loyal Manchester United supporter – like her father and uncles before her. We never knew Mama's father. He died before we were born. But, like her father, Mama said, she too believed that United could do no wrong. When David Beckham transferred to Real Madrid, she saw it as a betrayal and took down all the posters of him wearing his red shirt that, until then, had kept watch over our mattress as we slept. Then she mourned.

Some facts and statistics about Manchester United that Mama taught us:

- Manchester United first won the European Cup in 1968.
- By 2003, they had won the FA Premier League eight times.
- Sir Alex Ferguson is their manager. He was knighted by the Queen of England at Buckingham Palace. Afterwards, he ate cucumber sandwiches and drank tea in the Palace rose gardens. Mama showed us the photos that she cut out and saved from the *Zimbabwe Herald*.
- My brother was named after George Best. Number-one Manchester United player until David Beckham came along.

'Whatever you do, never confuse Manchester United with Manchester City, my children,' Mama would say. 'That is like confusing a thoroughbred horse with a village donkey. Understand?'

Manchester United rhymes with 'We're never tired'. Mama said their players are young lions. They play and play until their opponents drop with exhaustion.

Before, when there was still the occasional English Premiership game aired on television, thanks to corporate sponsorship and what-what, she would close the tavern early and hurry next door to sit herself down in front of our black-and-white television, which had pride of place on a small table in the living room. Together, the three of us would watch as Beckham worked his magic on the pitch.

'What a pass! There is nothing that this blessed white boy cannot do. Go! Run! Run!' Sometimes Mama would get so excited she would spill her mug of tea.

'Mama, they cannot hear you, you know. They are very far away.'

'Shhh, George. Now look at this mess. Chipo, fetch a rag, please, quick-quick. How do you know what they can and cannot hear, hey? He can feel that I am on his side, praying for him to thrash this manure Chelsea team.'

The minibus's windows are rattling. A young woman with a baby on her lap is snoring. But this is now, Chipo, I tell my reflection. Mama has been dead for almost three years, and only those like the General, who can afford satellite television, are able these days to keep abreast of the latest overseas soccer matches. And as for David Beckham, he certainly gives no thought to someone like me.

Two

Preparations to go. Four days. Documents. New cellphone. Peter and David's number scribbled down in several places and kept close. Food – buy what you can. Two packets of biscuits. Sell what you can. Avoid the General's man who comes to the house and bangs on the door so hard that the tin roof rattles. He demands, 'Why didn't you come to work? General wants to talk to you.' Pretend you are Mama hidden beneath a blanket, sick – TB, George says, to scare the man off. Don't let him in – don't tell anyone you are going.

No goodbyes – you need to slip away without honouring the rent that is due. Just one goodbye, one farewell. Your mother's grave. You go, you kneel at the mound with its wooden cross, gravel and metal bottle tops biting into your knees. Goodbye, goodbye. G-o-o-d-b-y-e, Mama.

I am sorry.

George and I are at the petrol station near the border post. We are looking for a truck driver willing to smuggle us for an agreed price. It is early evening. Six o'clock. The air has cooled. Soon it will be dark. That is what we want, says George. The night to hide us, the way a wild animal conceals its young in secret crevices. George goes to speak with another group of drivers who are smoking their cigarettes away from the pumps. I wait with the suitcase and watch the strangers pass on foot. There is a long queue of drivers waiting to fill their tanks, and many people with luggage and packages. The air smells of diesel. The word diesel sounds a bit like the word lethal.

Last night Mama's spirit visited me again. Not as she was when she was healthy and happy, charming and commanding her patrons around Old Trafford. No. How she always comes. With all the meat devoured from her bones like a famine victim. Teeth too large for her shrunken face. In my dream I tried to comfort her. She always looks so confused.

'What has happened to me, daughter?' Her bewildered eyes seemed to ask. But I have no words to satisfy the dead. No answers either. Three years ago, neither did the exhausted doctor and nurses at the local clinic.

'We can do no more for her here,' they said. 'We have no medicines, we haven't even been paid ourselves in five months. Perhaps if you could get her to Harare...'

Harare? George and I looked at each other. How? We could never afford that. Mama's eyes were closed. Was she listening?

The doctor sighed. 'Look, even if you could...' He did not finish his sentence. 'I am sorry.' He went to a cupboard and gave us a few tablets. 'Paracetamol for the pain,' he said, and sent her home. He was not unkind, only out of options, like the rest of us.

By then, Mama was so light I could carry her on my back as though she were a child. I remember her hot breath on my neck as she slipped in and out of consciousness. I had to hold onto her. And then those final months. When I would give her a sponge bath, my hands working so softly you would think she was a newborn baby. I remember her protruding ribs. Rasping gasps. Every day I fed her porridge water with a spoon that she spat and vomited out. Slowly, slowly the mother we knew disappeared. Day by day we grew closer to becoming orphans. Standing next to the petrol station, I bite my lip. Tell myself: think of something else.

Like the General's wife. Last night George told me that the General has thrown her out onto the street.

'Taught her a good lesson. No more monkey business for her,' George declared, with some satisfaction.

A woman with a large *tshangani* bag on her head passes. She is walking slowly, like someone walking on shifting sand instead of concrete. Her right hand is balancing her load. Looks heavy. Our own suitcase contains some clothes, my umbrella, biscuits for the journey and two one-litre bottles of water. It is small enough for me to carry it on my own without too much trouble. I watch the woman with the *tshangani* bag cross the road. Soon she will be gone from view and I want to shout after her: 'What is your life like there?' But I don't have the courage.

'Tortoise!' George signals for me to join him beside a red truck.

The truck driver is small and muscular, with grey stubble. He is Ndebele, not Shona like us. He says he is travelling almost all the way to our destination, and that George and I can sit in the main cab with him. After exchanging the traditional greetings and asking our names, he immediately begins to talk.

'Ah, they say you need no entry documents at the moment, but the border police do not care. If you have no passport and no visa they will not let you through. Not unless you give them something in return.'

Seeing our despair, he laughs, 'But do not worry, I will help you. You are very fortunate that I am the one who picked you up. There are plenty of thieves about. They take your money but hand you over to the police. And those border police, they will rob you before they throw you into jail. And even if you somehow manage to escape them, there are the *magumaguma* gangs. Know what those are?'

He does not wait for my brother and I to reply that we have already heard all about those terrible criminals.

'Young men. Zimbabwean or South African. They roam the two borders, looking for unfortunates like yourselves. If they find you, they rob you, beat you, rape or even kill you, or sell you into slavery for other gangs. And you…,' he said, turning from the wheel to look at me for a moment, 'you, they will take your organs, chop them out and sell them to the *muti* men. Ha ha ha. Yes, you are very lucky to have met me.' The truck driver laughs again. 'But tell me, *sisi*. Is it true that you people do not die, only disappear?'

That is what many believe about albinos. I blush and say nothing. The driver does not seem to mind and continues to tell us his horrible stories.

'Yes, you two are very fortunate to have found me. Very, very fortunate.'

'Don't move! Don't even breathe!'

The driver's warnings kick inside our heads as the border guards' flashlights sweep the inside of the truck cab. They are searching for stowaways. They are searching for us. We hold our breath. The mattress under which we are buried smells of sweat, beer and unwashed bodies. I want to retch. Something is biting my arms and now crawling towards my neck. Lice? Lice rhymes with nice, but there is nothing nice about them. Only bad.

Let them bite. They can eat me alive, I think to myself, if it means we will not be discovered. The guards are asking the driver lots of questions. He has climbed down and is standing outside. They want him to open the back.

If we are found, the driver has warned us, we will have to fork out a hefty bribe. Two hundred South African rand. Too much, George said. We cannot afford it. So we hold our breaths as though we are underwater. Under the rushing current of the Limpopo River. Until our lungs burn. And I can taste Limpopo River mud, sweet and earthy, and feel the hungry crocodiles swimming closer. Try to imagine something else. This driver at home? His family? On the dashboard there is a photo. Six children, girls of different ages. Neat school uniforms. Smiling proudly. And a wife. Must be why he agrees to take travellers like us. Not only for money. For some company. Better than talking to the road, to oblivious stars, to yourself, I tell myself as I try not to think about the border guards, about getting caught. Lonely. Lonely because you are the only. The only one. I am the only *sope* I know. Is that why I am lonely? And the driver? Must be lonely for him, too. To drive all day, all night. No wife. Children growing taller and ready for marriage. Without you. The flashlights pass here, pass there. My heart pounds. A crocodile is approaching.

I am a child afraid of the dark who wants to call out for her mother. Instead I can only pray to her spirit. Help us. Please. I do not want to go to prison, to rot away like a dead dog. I do not want to be raped.

The muttering border guards prod and poke. They are giving up. The hungry crocodiles glide past, their jaws still shut. We are safe. For the moment. Disappointed, the Zimbabwean guards raise the boom and wave the driver on. Somehow, after a similar game of cat and mouse, we manage to pass through on the South African side as well.

~

When the doctors sent Mama home to die, George fetched Mai Patricia, the *nganga*. We knew that Mama would probably not like it. She had no time for witch doctors. But we were desperate.

Mai Patricia came to our home and, after casting a sideways glance at me, squatted on the ground and threw her bones in front of Mama's sickbed. By now Mama was too feverish to protest, or perhaps even to notice. Peering down at the bones' secret message, Mai Patricia shook her head and sucked at the gap between her front teeth. George and I waited to hear what the *mudzimu* had to tell us.

'Your mother's disease goes back a long time. She is dying of an old wound to her heart.'

Mai Patricia did not look at me as she said this, but I knew she believed I had a part to play.

First, there was my father. When I was born, he took one look at my foreign pink form and condemned Mama for cheating on him with a white man. No amount of pleading on Mama's part or on the part of her relatives or even on the part of the midwife who assisted with the birth could convince him otherwise. My pale skin was the product of an interracial betrayal, pure and simple. Two days later, he was gone. We never heard from him again, but rumours came that he had taken up with a new wife in Harare who ran a small tuck shop not far from the Central Post Office. As for Mama, she always claimed that she was better off without him: 'Goodbye to rotten rubbish.' But it took many years before she was ready to love again.

Then came Stanley Mupfudza. I was six and George nine. Stanley was much older than our mother and worked for a local company distributing seeds and equipment to farms. He had small hands and a loud laugh and was a customer in Mama's tavern.

'But he supports *Everton*,' my brother complained after Stanley's first visit.

'I know,' Mama told us as she plumped up the cushions on the armchair where Stanley had been sitting. 'But you will see children. He will support United by the time we are through with him.'

Stanley the Everton Supporter starts to spend nights at our house. For Mama, he brings perfume and Oil of Olay, as well as meat that he gets from farmers. Together they disappear into Mama's room as George and I eat the sweets he has brought for us. Raspberry and caramel dissolve on our tongues and make our hearts swirl with pleasure. Dizzy fizzy. Fizzy sweets send a child's heart dizzy. Afterwards, over cups of tea, he quizzes George on his times tables.

'Six times twelve?'

'Seventy-two, Va Mupfudza.'

'Very good. You are a smart boy. You will go far.'

After his initial doubts, George decided he liked Stanley and his gifts, even though Stanley had yet to embrace Manchester United. George started to look forward to his visits.

'When Stanley and Mama marry,' George said to Michael one day, 'he and I will go fishing.' George had seen a TV programme in which a father and son went fishing together, and for weeks afterwards it was all he spoke about. Him and Stanley fishing.

'Black kids don't go fishing with their fathers for pleasure,' said Michael. 'That is what whites do.' Michael and George's debate continued. Growing bored, I took my umbrella, a Christmas gift from Mama, and went outside to check on our chickens, who had recently hatched six chicks, soft as cotton wool.

But Stanley was not what he seemed. One day I saw him leaving church with a woman and a boy. That woman looked nothing like Mama. She was tall and slim, except for the bump where another baby was growing. She did not wear colours as Mama liked to do, especially Manchester United red, but was dressed in a serious, stiff blue and grey skirt and jacket, like a headmistress or Sunday-school teacher. So Mama was Stanley's small house. I knew she could not have known it. What to do?

When Mai Mupfudza saw me looking, she spat at her feet and turned her back on me. It was local superstition – spit and you will protect your unborn child from catching the *sope*'s curse.

'Ugly monkey, what you staring at?' Stanley Mupfudza's young son bent down and picked up a stone to throw. I tried to dodge it, but it caught my cheek as I turned. After that I ran all the way back home.

'Nay! Chipo, you must be more careful. You know you are not like other children,' said Mama.

I was too miserable to defend myself. I barely felt the sting of the pungent-smelling Dettol on my skin. How could I tell Mama what I had seen or what Stanley's son had done? And how could I tell her that Stanley was already married and so was shaming Mama in the eyes of everybody.

'Such a baby, Chipo. It is only a small scratch.' Mama's voice softened. She put her hand on my head to calm my tears.

Stanley came to the house only once more after that. He and Mama went into her bedroom, and I went and hid outside behind the chomolia plants. Through the open window I could hear snatches of their conversation.

'I would leave my wife, Grace, but…'

I could not bear to hear Stanley say that I was the problem. Grace rhymes with face. It is my face he doesn't want close. So I went to stand at the edge of the road like someone waiting for something or someone important to arrive. But I was waiting for nothing. Mama and Stanley did not stay inside for long. When Stanley drove off, he did not wave goodbye. George turned off the video of Manchester United versus Chelsea at Wembley in 1994 in the FA Cup Final. It was his favourite, and Brian McClair was about to score the winning goal just a few minutes before the final whistle. George ran outside to watch Stanley's car recede in a cloud of goodbye-forever dust. I watched it go, too.

'Why is Va Stanley going?' Suddenly, as though reading my mind, George pointed at me and bared his teeth. 'It is because of *her*.'

'Shut your mouth, George!' Mama snapped. It was rare for her to lose her temper with us, and George ran away, probably to Michael's. That was where George always went when he was in trouble at home. He did not come back until suppertime had passed and it was dark.

'Come here, Chipo.' Mama called me to her. She told me to take off my jersey so that she could rub lotion onto my skin. She did not mention Stanley the Everton Supporter again. But I knew George was right. I was the one responsible for breaking Mama's heart twice.

Three

'The seven thirty-five train for Athlone will be delayed by twenty minutes. Platform two.'

Half past seven in the morning, 2 October 2009. There are two hundred and forty-two days until the start of the World Cup. Two days since we left behind all we have ever known. My bladder is bursting, but George says, 'You can't go to the toilet, Michael's cousins will be here soon.'

Everywhere, people. Some look sleepy, others harassed, eager to be out of this crowded train terminal that is busier than a termite hill. South Africans look different from Zimbabweans, that is for sure. Plumper. Ordinary people back home, those not wealthy like the General and the Mistress, are thin like green maize shoots. But here they are more like well-fed cattle. Two women waddle past, clutching their handbags. One has bought a packet of Nik-Naks. A robust-looking man walks quickly as he talks on his cellphone. In his free hand he holds a paper cup of steaming tea or coffee.

My stomach rumbles. I am hungry. We have not eaten anything for almost a day since our biscuits ran out.

'Try to at least look like you know what you are doing and not like a country girl holding a hoe.'

George's words come out all distorted. His jaw is still swollen from where the driver slapped him.

When we were a safe distance from the border, the driver let us climb out from under his stinking blankets. It was dark. Just a half-moon. Its watery yellow glow was not enough to see by. So our first vision of South Africa was of little more than shadows, punctuated by the lights of passing vehicles. But I could smell the bush. Dry tree roots and peppery sap.

Now that we have crossed the border, the driver is silent. No more talk. No more stories. Just the sound of the truck growling beneath us, its aged suspension bumping over the dips as we turn off the main highway onto a dirt road. Suddenly the driver stops the truck and turns off the ignition. There, in the darkness of the bush, with the crickets, it seems, crying out for our help, he turns to George and demands more money.

'But we agreed,' my brother protests.

'After the risk I just took for you? Both of you must get out now!'

Terrified, I close my eyes. Meanwhile, my normally proud brother begs: 'Please, baba, we are poor orphans.'

'No, you are ungrateful lumps of shit! Get out!'

The once-friendly driver has become another man. A heated conversation follows. The driver demanding and shouting. George grovelling and begging.

Finally: 'How much do you have?'

I do not hear what my brother mumbles.

'Just give it to me.'

My brother hands over the notes. I know he has a few more in his sock, but thankfully the driver does not know about that.

'Is this all you have? For this pathetic amount you two can stay in the back!'

Then, before my brother can move, the driver gives him an angry smack on the side of the head.

We both climb out of the front cab and go to the back of the truck. The driver slams the container door shut with a terrible bang and locks us in from the outside, leaving us in total darkness.

We are prisoners, I think. We huddle together among the crates of unripe avocados. We are prisoners. And with that thought come memories. The thud-thud of the soil landing on top of Mama's coffin. Sand in my shoes. Auntie Ruth's wailing. Uncle Charles's perspiration on his brow, the back of his shirt darkening as he shovels. Mama. You are trapped.

I will go mad in here, I think. The truck bumps over a pothole and my side slams into the sharp corner of a crate. But just as I feel the darkness closing in, George takes my hand and squeezes it so tight that I know he too is terrified. I feel my heartbeat begin to slow.

Over the next few hours, the driver stopped twice, but he didn't let us out. When he finally did, we saw that a young woman and two young men had taken our places in the front cab. They did not make eye contact with us as we all hurried into the bush to empty our bladders and bowels while the driver smoked a cigarette. George's jaw was already badly bruised and swollen.

'Is your jaw very sore?' I whisper. I want to reach out to touch George again, but in the daylight of Cape Town station he flinches from my touch.

'Shut up, Chipo. Look out for—' My brother's words are drowned out by another train announcement. Mitchell's Plain. Departing. Platform Four.

I look down at my crumpled skirt and the suitcase lodged between my legs. With my hands I try to smooth the creases. Inside that truck we took comfort from the smell of each other's perspiration, like flour mixed with water and yeast, left to ferment in a tin shack in the noonday heat. It was the smell of fear, yes, but also a reminder that we were still alive. But now I feel only dirty.

'Thank God. It's them.'

I look up in the station and see two men approaching. City men. Tall. Both wearing sunglasses, T-shirts, jeans, and sneakers. Identical. Yes, identical twins, but not the same. Look closer, Chipo, I tell myself. Behind the sunglasses of one, his left eyelid hangs low. An injury from when he was a boy and he fell from the bicycle he used to charge the other children to ride. That is Peter. The other, with warm smiling eyes like Andy Cole, is David. He never teased you when the other children did and often shared his lunch with the stray dogs waiting on the other side of the school fence, hoping for scraps. All the girls, too. Hoping for scraps of David's attention. His affections. And you, Chipo? Do you forget how you used to leave the house a half-hour early, hoping just to touch David's shadow with the tip of your shoe as he walked to school?

When they see George they wave and hurry forwards. Warm embraces, 'Welcome to Cape Town, George. You've grown. You used to be short! But what happened to your face?'

As an afterthought, they turn to me. A sigh from Peter. A smile and a nod from David, who reaches down to take our suitcase. Then the three move off, still laughing and joking, lost in catching up.

'Our building is called "President's Heights". It is taller than almost the tallest in Harare, and of course much taller than anything you ever saw in Beitbridge. From our room, we look over the city and can even glimpse Signal Hill,' Peter says.

However, when we approach, George and I immediately recognise that this is not the sort of building that any president we know of will choose to reside. There is washing hanging from every window and the mismatched curtains flap like tattered flags in the wind, and groups of young men loiter near the entrance with, it seems, nothing to do to pass their time but smoke and stand about talking. Still, we are lucky, I tell myself. Lucky to have David and Peter. Friends once, so friends still? Yes. At least, not strangers. And you should be grateful, Chipo. They could have told George that they would not take you too.

One by one, through a clicking turnstile, we enter. Into a wide, gloomy lobby. Inside, a hundred post boxes stuffed with rubbish.

'Do not receive post here, not unless you want it stolen.'

Normally, Peter explains, it is tricky for African foreigners like ourselves to find places to stay. Most landlords require a South African ID, which, if you are a foreigner waiting for your papers, you do not have. Also proof of employment, bank account details, and so on and so forth. And a large deposit. But this building is different. Here, Peter tells us, the landlords let the African foreigners bypass the usual procedures – for a price. Peter rubs his thumb against his slim index finger like he is toying with a shred of tobacco.

We are in the belly of President's Heights, situated in the heart of Long Street, a street that runs like a spinal column through the city centre, almost down to the ice-cold Atlantic. President's Heights and Long Street. Long Street and President's Heights. iKapa. The Mother City. All That's Pretty. iKapa The Mother City A Place Without Pity.

~

I lift my skirt and squat. There is no toilet seat and my flip-flops stick to the lino. There is no way I'm setting my buttocks down on this porcelain, I think. And the lino could do with a good scrub, too. Still, it is a relief to finally unburden my bladder. Maybe later, when I am not so tired, I will wash this whole room down. When I come out of the bathroom, I find George sitting on a white plastic chair at the plastic table in the brothers' room, eating a bowl of mealie porridge that the brothers have reheated.

This one room on the seventh floor is to be our home. One room for four. I look around. In the far left corner there is a stove and a sink and one shelf on which sits a small bag of maize, a bag of salt, a kilo bag of sugar, a box of tea and a few pots and pans. Apart from the plastic garden table with three chairs, there are two mattresses covered with blankets on the floor, a green metal chest under the window and a wardrobe with no door. A sheet of plastic protects its contents. Next to the wardrobe there are four pairs of shoes lined up neatly against the wall.

'Eat, Chipo,' David says kindly. I blush as I serve myself a few spoonfuls. I do not want to appear greedy. To be greedy is not ladylike. That is what Mama always told me. I want to appear ladylike in front of David. I am glad that I have washed my hands and face.

I take my plate of food and go and sit on the floor under the window. The carpet, although marked with stains in many places, feels soft against my legs.

The mealie porridge is only lukewarm but still delicious in the way that food always is whenever you are extremely hungry. After we have eaten, I pack the dishes into the sink in the corner of the room. Then I roll up my sleeves to begin to wash. A lady knows when to do the men's dishes. But Peter says wait, you can do that later. First he and David want to take us back down onto Long Street to show us around. He says he will begin to introduce George to other Zimbabweans who can help with finding work.

'And our suitcase with the Congolese fellow? Is it safe to leave it?' asks George.

David and Peter have explained that the bedroom in the flat is rented by a Congolese tailor.

I had noticed that the door nearest to the front door was closed, and had wondered who or what was inside. Coming from that room there is a delicious aroma, intoxicating as the scent of beef gravy.

'Congolese?' my brother had asked, surprised. 'Why doesn't he live with his own people?'

'Long story,' said David in a low voice as he unlocked the front door. 'But don't worry. The noise of his sewing machine – that is as much as you will know of him from one day to the next. He cooks, eats and even washes in his own room.'

'And, most importantly, he is willing to pay the lion's share of the rent,' explained Peter.

'He is an honest fellow. You can leave it,' David says now.

If David says so, I feel confident. I take out my umbrella and follow.

I lie in bed, unable to fall asleep. It is late. Well after midnight. Peter and David are snoring on one side of the room, where they have pushed aside the table and chairs and lowered their mattress. I count their breaths, one and two, in and out. I count until I reach a hundred and twenty, but my mind is not yet heavy and loose. George is asleep too, beside me. David has said we can share his mattress until we find our own.

'If you go out early in the morning, up to where the nice houses are below the mountain, sometimes people have thrown them out. Otherwise you will have to go to the second-hand furniture shops in Woodstock.'

I am not the only one in President's Heights who cannot find peace. Beyond the thin walls and floors, ceilings too, televisions and stereos blare. I turn on my side and Peter's words earlier in the day return: 'This is your home now. Pay close attention. See this Mountain Dew tuck shop? They call them *spaza* shops here. It is owned by the Somalis. They keep to themselves. You won't secure a position with them. They only employ family or Xhosa-speaking locals.'

We continue on. One small shop sells sports clothes, another jewellery, another furniture. All still closed. Waiting for nine o'clock, David explains. George looks pleased. Isn't this what he promised? Shops packed with the heart's desires?

At each important point along Long Street, Peter and David stop and explain what is what. There seems to be nothing they don't know. It is like they were born here. But I feel dizzy from all this newness. Dizzy rhymes with fizzy.

'Here is the bead shop where I work. Next door is Atkinson's Antiques. Two old whites run it. Next door, Clarke's bookshop.'

At that moment a tall, handsome African man passes, a black baton hanging from his belt. He looks with suspicion at Peter and David. I step closer to George and lower my umbrella.

'From the Congo,' Peter whispers when the man is no longer in earshot. 'DRC people do all the security for these shops. They are also most of the parking marshals around here. You will find it is like that in Cape Town. Certain nationalities, certain jobs.'

My brother frowns. Says nothing.

'The meat and boerewors carts are owned by locals. They come at night and sell food to the people who are here for a good time. By morning they are gone. But the glass empties and cardboard abandoned by the carts, as well as by all these bars and cafés, they belong to them…'

'Who?' George asks.

'Them.'

We all look. Peter points across the street to the alleyway we have just passed, where three sitting men appear to be dozing. One is white; the other two, David explains, are called 'coloureds', although it is difficult to tell them apart. The white man's skin is dark from spending every day outdoors. All three, like strange brothers, have untidy beards, woollen hats and overcoats in spite of the heat.

'The white man, he is called Kobus. He and his friends, they are in charge of collecting the cardboard boxes and empties from the bars and organising them for the municipality every morning. They are locals. Drunks. They sleep on the street and spend all that they make on bad rum. They buy it at the liquor shop at the top of the street. An old white man runs the shop with his son. They never give credit but will sell to anyone, and their beer is good value.'

'So what are we Zimbabweans supposed to do?' I can see George is beginning to worry, but doesn't want to show it. 'What are *our* jobs?'

David shrugs, 'Mostly waiters and chefs. Sometimes cleaners. Sometimes shop assistants.'

Nationalities sounds like irrationalities. I turn again. Still no sleep. Peter is snoring louder now. David joins in. Below, Long Street is more alive than ever. Every unfamiliar sound reminds me of Peter's warning that life in Cape Town is different from what we knew back home and that we must be on our guard. A man is singing in a language I cannot understand. He is singing for the girl he loves as they walk to a bar. That is what I tell myself. A group of young women chatter excitedly, then laugh. They speak English but are not Zimbabwean. I imagine them dressed in bright dresses, their clothes smelling of perfume, their skin of Nivea. Their skin is spotless and pure, no doubt, like expensive milk chocolate. The smooth sort that comes wrapped in gold foil and says 'Nestlé' on the packet. I am sure they are university students, or secretaries working in the sparkling glass office blocks that you can see from our window. I have never seen so many windows in single buildings.

Then I hear, 'Yoyoyoyoy! Give-me-back-my-fucking-cell-phone-battery!' This is followed by 'She, she is the one who took it!' The argument moves up the street and out of earshot. I hear passing motorbikes, and then police sirens. A car hoots. A truck farts its sooty puffs beneath our window.

The truck's rumble takes me back to the border. Suddenly a lump of fear forms in my stomach. *Will* we be able to make a go of life here, like Peter and David seem to be? You are here now, Chipo, you *must* find a way. You *will* find a way. I whisper the words into the darkness like a soothing prayer. You must find a way. You will find a way. You must, you will, you must, you will.

George smacks his lips next to me. Worn out, I roll next to him and push my body as close as I can without the risk of waking him. Stop worrying and go to sleep, Chipo, I tell myself. Sleep sleep sleep.

Four

Before illness robbed Mama of her strength, she was known for her resourcefulness. As well as owning and running Old Trafford, she also recorded all of the televised Premier League matches on her VHS machine. Then, when the league was having its summer break, Mama would carry our television outside and, using a long extension lead, transform Old Trafford's front yard into a place to re-watch all of our favourite matches.

I was always amazed at how many people would pay to watch soccer matches when they already knew who would win, hearts bursting with pride, and who would lose and leave the pitch with their tails between their legs. On those mild winter evenings our backyard did brisk business. George would sell beers and plates of stew, roasted peanuts still warm in their shells, and other refreshments. I would be in charge of making sure that only those who had paid were allowed entrance. If the person did not want me to touch their money, then my mother would send them packing.

When they were boys and teenagers, George, Peter, David and Michael played soccer every weekend and most evenings too, on dry fields after the harvest, or up and down streets, or even at the sides of roads as the cars and trucks passed. This is how they enjoyed their free time, because for soccer you do not need much.

Not even a proper ball. Almost anything round will do, and boys are ingenious with their inventions. Balls were made from rags, or from tightly compressed plastic bags. My brother and his friends favoured the five-kilogram bags of mealie meal. If the ball begins to unravel, then play must stop until it is retied. And the goals? Two planks, propped up however. Back in Luthumba, long after David and Peter had moved to Harare with their parents and George and Michael had started spending their time in the tavern rather than on the soccer pitch, if you stood in the doorway of our home in the evening, you could still see skinny barefoot boys skidding and kicking up red dirt. At home their food cupboards were no doubt empty and they were in need of school fees and books. But for the moment, all worries were forgotten. They were Michael Owen, David Beckham or that Brazilian, Ronaldo.

'Goal! Goal!' they shout. A boy not older than ten, the scorer of the goal, does his victorious backflip.

'If some of the wives would come to my tavern, they would not recognise their husbands,' Mama would often joke. 'With Seven Days and a soccer game to watch, the lame husband can dance, the deaf husband can hear every whistle blast. A place of miracles.' She put her hands on her hips. 'If only the pastor at the New Jerusalem Church talked more soccer and less fire and brimstone, his church would be packed to the rafters!'

When we arrive in Cape Town it is clear the soccer fever, which we knew so well in our own house, is slowly gripping an entire nation and even a continent, even though the World Cup itself will not start for another seven months. We read about it every day in the newspapers that David brings home after work. One day he also brings home a calendar. I do not know where he got it from and he does not tell us. Only that it is for counting down the days until the start of the World Cup. On the cover it says: IT'S TIME. CELEBRATE AFRICA'S HUMANITY.

'That's the motto. What they are putting on the T-shirts and posters.'

At the end of each week, David counts how many days remain until the World Cup arrives in Cape Town and the other major South African cities. Just two hundred and thirty, with much to look forward to in between, including, at the end of November, David tells us one evening, the team draw.

'But first,' Peter says, pointing at George and me with his fork, 'you two will have to survive Home Affairs.'

Why did you leave your home country?

Three forty-five in the morning. A full moon. We are already on our way to Home Affairs for our second visit in one week. The first time we went, George ignored Peter and David's warnings to go early or even sleep in the queue the night before to ensure we are seen to.

'I didn't leave Zimbabwe to sleep on the street in South Africa like a stray dog,' George had said. 'Enough that I must do the job of a maid.'

With the help of Zimbabwean friends of Peter and David, George had found a position in the kitchens of a Mexican restaurant on Long Street, called Tortilla, cleaning plates and mopping floors.

'Do not complain,' David told him after his first evening of work. 'What did you think? That a company would snap you up and make you CEO? You know Isaiah, the tall waiter from Senegal? An accountant back home. And the other new fellow, Jeremiah? They say he was studying for a master's in electrical engineering at the University of Zimbabwe! That's how it starts for us. At the bottom. With time, God willing, our fortunes will improve.'

Arriving at the Home Affairs office in Maitland an hour and a half later, we learnt our lesson. The queue reached all the way back to Lagos, Harare, Kinshasa. So this time we are taking no chances. As we walk, the last of the Long Street revellers are hungrily gobbling down boerewors rolls and kebabs that they have bought just as the food stalls are closing. George yawns. He doesn't bother to put his hand up to cover his mouth. If Mama were here, she would tell him off for lax manners.

My feet are cold, my body shivering. From the pre-dawn chill, yes, but also from anxiety. Anxiety does not rhyme or sound like anything. It is unique and terrible. And George? He is anxious, too. His right hand fidgets with the pack of cigarettes in his pocket like he has something to hide. I have heard that trips to Home Affairs are what every African immigrant in South Africa dreads most. The only thing he dreads more is the police.

Last night, David and Peter spent a long time reminding us of what we must and must not do and say. They made us repeat all the answers for the officials' questions until they were satisfied.

Name?

Date of birth?

Place of origin?

Why did you leave your home country?

'This is the most important question. Do not tell them you have come here to look for a job. Starvation will not get you a temporary asylum-seeker's permit. Tell them you were politically active with the opposition party and feared for your life.'

They gave us some names of opposition-party members and dates when the government cracked down on MDC rallies and made arrests.

'If you are lucky, eventually you will receive refugee status.'

Refugee sounds like flea. That is how, we are warned, many at Home Affairs view us. Like fleas that need to have their heads squeezed off.

'Remember, Home Affairs officials like to lead us African foreigners up the garden path. So don't lose your temper. And whatever you do, don't give them a bribe. They will ask, but in the end they will do nothing for you.'

When we arrived at the Maitland building the first time, we saw a large sign saying Zimbabweans will be served only on Thursdays from nine to twelve and on Mondays from nine to eleven-thirty. Malawians and Nigerians on Wednesdays nine to twelve. Somalis on Fridays nine to twelve, and so on. Thankfully we knew about this and had come on the correct day.

Here is what happens when you reach Home Affairs: you wait. Eventually an official comes. His voice reminds me of the voices of the border guards. He doesn't talk to us; he shouts. I begin to sweat and my stomach is cramping. The first ten, he says, 'Go in!' The rest must continue to wait. Those who are rich enough to pay an agent on their behalf are lucky because those agents seem to have an arrangement with the officials. They pass directly through the doors to the front of the queues with their piles of passports and paperwork. The poor, like George and I, must wait – me in the queue for women, George in the queue for men. The first time, we never made it past those front doors. The second time, arriving much earlier, we are more fortunate.

Patience is a virtue. Isn't that what they say? I watch my brother's queue move more quickly than mine. I am afraid. Will I be left behind? Hours pass. One form, then another and another. And all the time, questions. The hands of the clock on the dirty white wall move onward. Overhead, a strip light buzzes and twitches as though nervous on our behalf. It is lunchtime. We have been queuing since five o'clock. But we are not yet finished.

What is a temporary asylum-seeker's permit? A magic piece of paper. It grants you permission to stay in South Africa while the government considers your permanent-residence application. All foreign Africans must carry it. Once they have a permit, most are so afraid they might lose it that they take it with them everywhere.

When I eventually come by one, I stare at the magic piece of paper. It does not look so very important, but it is. I read it once, twice, three times.

I look so shy behind my thick spectacles. My hair and eyelashes – so white. Yellow like custard powder, just add water, George used to say when we were children. I remember how the bright lights made me squint even more than usual, and the photographer's gruff instructions made me especially nervous.

'Face forwards. Look at the camera. Don't smile.'

My current sun rash – is it really as bad as this? I hold the paper at the tip of my nose and squint through my glasses like a scientist trying to find a hidden virus through his microscope.

Who is this girl? Who is Chipo Nyamubaya? I think to myself as I examine the document. Before I can decide, George pulls the paper from my hands.

'You are bound to lose it.' He folds the permit and puts it in his wallet for safekeeping. 'Without this piece of paper,' he warns, 'the police will arrest you and deport you, no questions asked. If there is a fire or any trouble, it is this piece of paper you must grab first. No one will try to help you if you do not have it. You cannot even buy a new cellphone without it.'

George's warnings are later reiterated by Peter. Last year, he tells us, a young Zimbabwean man died of starvation after waiting for weeks to be seen by Home Affairs. It was reported in the newspapers.

'That was when Home Affairs was still at the Foreshore. Afterwards they moved it far away to Bellville, Maitland. People waited so long in the queues that a squatter town of sorts sprang up. It was terrible. The man was supposed to be staying in this very building, but he dropped dead while standing in the queue outside Home Affairs. He had returned day after day for months. Each time he was turned away, told to come again tomorrow, next week, in two weeks. So eventually in desperation he just stayed and eventually starved.'

Afterwards, I cannot get Peter's terrible story out of my head. That night, as I lie in bed trying to fall asleep, there is a commotion on Long Street. Blue lights bounce off the walls in our room. But all I can think of is a man as thin as Limpopo-river reeds. His body is so light from hunger it can no longer weigh itself down. So it floats, lost to the wind. It is carried over the Foreshore and up into the city. Looking down, confused, he asks himself: 'What is going on? I am losing my place in the queue!'

Only when he is hovering above President's Heights, looking down at the pigeon shit and feathers on the roof, does he realise he is dead.

Five

David is reading a book he found at the restaurant where he works. A tourist forgot it and the manager said he could keep it. It is called *The Death of Shaka Zulu*. David is devouring it. I am stirring the *sadza*, waiting for the pale maize grains to grow stiff and darken in colour so that I know they are ready. George and I have been in Cape Town for four weeks and life has fallen into a sort of routine, although tonight it is just David and myself in our flat. Peter and George are out, following up the possibility of a better-paying job for George at a small café where they have heard the owner is looking for waiters.

'Is it true that you did your legal studies back in Harare?'

David nods and turns another page. With no sofa to sit on, he has put a pillow behind his back and is lying on the floor, his back against the wall.

'Yes, but what good was it?' he replies. 'I didn't have the money to bribe my way into a firm to do my articles, and jobs were so scarce that I couldn't even find work at a supermarket.' David looks up from his book for a moment. 'I remember you were very diligent in your studies. I am sure you were an A-grade student…'

I blush with pleasure and massage the *sadza* with the wooden spoon. Nearly ready. But my proud moment is short-lived.

'Grade A? Chipo? Ha ha. A good joke.' My brother. How could I not have heard him come in? I look at him. Immediately it is clear that his job search has failed to bear fruit. He is in a foul mood.

'Yes, A-grade for scrub, cook and clean. Speaking of which, why is dinner not ready yet, hey? Can't you even manage that, Tortoise?'

He flops down onto our mattress and tugs at his laces.

'Oh shit!' George's face crumples with disgust. He has trodden in vomit on the dark stairs of President's Heights.

'Bloody drunk Congolese bastards!' He holds out one sneaker, then the other, for me to take: 'Tortoise, quick!'

It was not George who first named me 'Tortoise'. I have my school peers to thank for that.

'Maaam, Chipo works like a tor-toise!'

I am twelve and it is the third week of my first term at secondary school. Mrs Guchu, the class teacher, sighs and, taking off her spectacles, rubs her eyes. She is a Christian woman who knows that the Scriptures say that Jesus favours the meek and mild, but sometimes it seems she is not so sure. The other learners grumble and fidget as I press my nose so close to the board that I can smell the chalk powder and the sour residue of the water used by learners on detention to wash the blackboards the previous day. Afterwards they must tip the water onto the school vegetable garden. My classmates groan and throw insults at my back like rotten eggs.

'Why must we all wait for her before continuing the task?'

'And I cannot see anything with her standing so close to the board.'

'She is blocking the middle lines!'

'Tortoisetortoisetortoise.'

Soon the whole class takes up the chant.

It makes me sweat with shame. But what am I supposed to do? This is the only way I can see what is written.

'Silence!' Mrs Guchu slams her palm on the board.

'Chipo, you must tell your mother to get you stronger spectacles if the ones you currently possess are inadequate. You cannot be allowed to delay the rest of the class. They are falling behind in their studies, and we have not even discussed osmosis or photo-synthesis yet.'

Impatiently, Mrs Guchu closes her worn, government-issued textbook and leads me to my desk.

'But it is not her spectacles,' my mother explained after school in the headmistress's office later that week. I stared down at the desk, wishing it would open its wooden jaws and swallow me, like a hippopotamus.

'It is the sunlight coming in through the windows. Her eyes are light-sensitive.'

'Are you suggesting the other pupils work in darkness in order to accommodate your daughter?'

'Of course not…'

'Or perhaps you would like the school to switch its schedule and conduct our lessons at night, by candlelight, so your daughter might better see the board? This isn't primary school any more, you know, Mrs Nyamubaya. Students must sit their O-levels in a few years' time and the pressure is on.' The headmistress folded her arms and pursed her lips.

My mother stood up. 'Come on, Chipo, we are going.'

Once outside, she straightened my sunhat and took my hand. I squinted up into her face. Concern simmered beneath anger: 'You will be all right. Just do your best.'

My best is to stay in class after the other learners have left for break, or even for home, and copy the teacher's blackboard notes in my own time. Sometimes, though, some of my fellow learners thought it a good joke to erase what was written before I had time to finish. It was David who came to my rescue, who chased them away. He carried some authority with the children my age.

There was one girl. Her name was Violet. Her father worked for local government in a modest position. But the whole family thought themselves the better for it. Violet always had sweets and chocolate that she shared only with her friends. Together they would sit in a circle and I would listen as the girls begged: 'Please Violet, just one small piece.' Taking her time, Violet would apportion their rations according to their degree of bottom-kissing. One day, Violet and her friends were sitting in the classroom during break. It was hot outside and they had ignored the school rules that said they must be out in the play yard. They were all chewing on the buttery toffees that Violet had finally apportioned – just one sticky toffee each, after much begging – when David came in.

'What are you lot doing in here? You know the rules.'

I began to pack up my things, my heart heavy. I would probably not have another chance to complete the notes on the board about Charles Dickens.

'No, not you,' said David gently. His smile like a glass of cool water. 'It is OK if you finish first, Chipo.'

'Not fair!' Violet and her friends puffed their cheeks in annoyance. They, of course, all had crushes on David. He shrugged and went out.

'Chipo thinks David is her boyfriend,' Violet hissed to her friends as they gathered their bags. Then, standing so close that I could smell the toffee still on her breath, she turned to me and spat: 'He only helps you because he feels sorry for you!' And, as she was leaving the room, 'No one will ever want to marry you, *sssssope!*' She and the other girls laughed like jackals.

The truth is that in spite of George's grand promises, in some ways life does not change much for me these first few weeks in Cape Town. In Beitbridge I cleaned for the General and his family, and cooked and cleaned at home for George and myself. In Cape Town I cook and clean for George, David and Peter. But I do not mind. Every day I do my work happily if I receive one of David's compliments. He is the only one who seems to notice what others take for granted.

'No one washes shirts like you, Chipo. The sweat stains are completely removed.'

And when I have swept or scrubbed the carpet, he always takes his shoes off before walking about so as not to give me extra work.

One day David was sitting on his mattress examining a pair of trousers whose inside thigh had worn through again and certainly could not be repaired a fifth time. 'No use. These cannot be patched up again,' I heard him say.

I was determined to find a solution. I had seen the sign on Jean-Paul's door advertising clothing repairs. Jean-Paul, it seemed, had a reputation as one of the best tailors around. Every day people brought him fabric to be sewn into something, or clothes to be altered and mended. Men and women. Mostly people from our building, but even some locals. When no one else was around, I pulled the pair of trousers out of the rubbish and hid them among my things. Once a day I would take them out and smell them. Soap flakes. Aftershave. This is how David's skin must smell, I told myself. I wondered what it would be like to be even an ant tickling that beautiful skin so that the hairs on David's arms stood on end.

Still, it took me several days to gather the courage to go and knock on Jean-Paul's door. It was a Friday morning in early November. If you are going to do it, Chipo, go now, I told myself, or throw them back into the rubbish, you stupid coward. I passed the area that acted as our kitchen and the bathroom and went down the short passage. My hand hovered for a moment. Then, closing my eyes and taking a deep breath, I knocked.

Six

'Yes, come in. Oh, it is you. Please put your finger here.'

I blink. The curtains are wide open, the room too bright. My eyes begin to water, and for a few seconds, until he moves away from the window, I cannot make out Jean-Paul clearly. He is just a voice, surrounded by a shimmering watery halo.

'Here.'

Shyly, I shield my eyes with one hand and approach. This is better than Home Affairs, I tell myself. What's the worst he can do?

'Put your finger here, please.' Jean-Paul is standing in front of a mannequin. He has folded the fabric onto it as though onto a body, and I can see now that he is making a dress for a woman with a body as round as a cooked bun.

I do as Jean-Paul asks, and watch as he slips a pin into the fabric. He continues to work, not asking yet why I have come, only directing me to hold the fabric in place where he needs to do his pinning for a sleeve, then lower, where there will later be a belt. It is only when he takes up his cane and steps around the mannequin that I notice that his left foot is lame. It does not move quickly and precisely like the right, but drags behind as though fast asleep.

As Jean-Paul works, I take in my surroundings. I have never seen anything quite like it before, not even on television or in the

General's wife's magazines. Everywhere there are pictures of Jesus Christ or some or other twinkling religious relic. In one corner of the room there seems to be a sort of altar. A small statue of the Virgin Mary and, beside it, a photograph of a smiling woman and a child. Also a vase of fresh yellow flowers.

Jean-Paul shakes his head.

'I do not know how I can be expected to get this done in time. The bride's dress, yes, but now three bridesmaids and one getting fatter by the day.'

Then, looking at me properly for the first time, 'You know, with your complexion you should avoid beige.'

He is referring to the simple cotton dress I am wearing. It is only one of three that I possess. Not the sort you would find in the General's wife's magazines or even on Jean-Paul's mannequin. Rather, they are what I have been able to buy on sale from the Chinaman shops. *Zhing-zhongs* all of them, of inferior quality, like so much of what those people sell.

'Do you want to live a life without colour? Like some housewife in the suburbs? Beige is for those types. You are an African. Try yellow instead or, better yet, blue.'

I nod. Will I actually find the courage to tell him why I have come? David's trousers are still under my arm.

Jean-Paul turns back to the dress taking shape on the mannequin. He is on his hands and knees now, measuring the hem with the tape measure that hangs around his neck. The cane he uses to help him walk is propped up against the table. For David's sake, I swallow and speak up.

'I have come about these. They belong to my roommate. Do you think you could mend them? They are very worn. I do not know how I can pay you, perhaps I could clean…'

Jean-Paul does not reply to my question. Instead, looking up at me from his position on his knees, he says: 'You know how I learnt English?'

I shake my head.

'There was a man. He taught me for free. He had been a teacher. Before…'

Before what? But Jean-Paul does not finish his sentence. With an effort he stands up, moves with his cane to the chair and sits down with a sigh behind his sewing machine. Then, gesturing to the trousers but not looking up at me as he pushes the pedal with his good foot: 'Leave them on the chair. You can pay me later.'

It is supposed to be the start of summer, but today there is only rain. It falls light like hospital gauze. Cape Town's rain-darkened sky can be all the shades of grey. Sometimes like wood smoke, sometimes dark as concrete. At other times it matches the pigeons that peck at Long Street's pavements, their feathers congealed with gurgling drain water. But now it is almost white. Our windows will not open properly, only a few centimetres. To keep the drunks and drug addicts from jumping to their deaths, Peter says. But still, I could spend hours standing here in front of it, watching the world below – especially when it rains. I find the smell of rain intoxicating. Like running my hands through a new bag of golden maize kernels. Like smelling freshly laundered clothes. Ever since I was a girl, I have felt that when it rains, some of my troubles are washed away with the dust and the dirt.

Three Congolese men are crossing Long Street. They jump the puddles as they cross in a gap between the traffic. Bright suit jackets over Dolce & Gabbana T-shirts and jeans, talking and gesticulating as they dodge the puddles that will ruin their narrow-toed, crocodile-leather shoes. David says that these smartly dressed Congolese are called 'sapeurs' and they will go without food before they allow themselves to look like poor immigrants.

'Vanity is the destroyer of kings,' Jeremiah has commented in the past. He likes to quote from the Bible. Especially the doom-and-gloom passages. Must be because of his name. People back home say the name you give your baby affects his character. Gift rhymes with shift. Sometimes I forget my name is Gift and think it is Tortoise instead.

'Everyone must find his way to survive,' David says in his new friend's defence whenever George or Peter criticise him. He has been inviting Jeremiah to visit sometimes after work, and my brother and Peter do not like it.

'But he is as dry as last week's toast!' protests Peter.

'He is not dry, brother. He is intelligent. Not everyone's world revolves around drinking and womanising, you know.'

David is that sort of man. Always willing to view others in their best light.

I turn back to the window. A woman with colourful dusters tucked under her left arm, and a plastic bag tied over her hair, is approaching from the other side of the road. She does not look Zimbabwean. From West or Central Africa, maybe? Congo or Senegal? She is coming home after trying to sell those dusters at traffic lights. Today she is also carrying a bag of shopping from Shoprite. I wonder what she has bought. Her hair is not short and tightly curled like mine, but very long and braided. She is thin and looks old enough to be the mother of many. Where does she come from? Another young woman. White. Wearing shorts and hurrying in the direction of Kloof Street. She looks wet. Her hair is tied back.

If this were a warm day, perhaps she would be on her way to catch a taxi to take her to the sea on the other side of the mountain. I have heard the ocean is as cold as plunging your hands into a bucket of ice, regardless of the weather.

The woman with the colourful dusters looks tired today. Must be difficult to sell such things when it rains. I have heard some of the people in our building complaining. No one wants to stop their cars or roll down the windows even when the weather is good. Everyone in this city is very concerned with crime, says David. I watch the woman slowly turn the corner into the alleyway that leads to the main entrance of President's Heights.

The others should be home soon. My pot of boiled sugar beans is ready on the stove. Beans and rice. One of David's favourites. Of course, he loves meat best. I wish I could afford to buy him meat. Even chicken thighs. I would cook them with a little paprika and spice. I love the colour of paprika. It is a passionate, joyful colour.

I close my eyes. The rain is coming down harder now. I imagine myself standing naked in the downpour, warm rainwater cleansing my face, my back, my arms, my legs. That early evening, as I stand alone in our room, I wonder who at that moment is listening to the rain rattling on their windows too and thinking, yes, I want to be standing in that. In Beitbridge the rain fell as rarely as an honest politician's words. Here, they say, just by looking at Table Mountain you can tell what the day's skies will bring. The rain means there will probably be fewer people going out to the Long Street bars tonight. I turn off the gas.

'Just kill it! Oh, for fuck's sake…'

A Saturday morning. Mid-November.

'What is going on?' I put down my bag of shopping.

'David has lost his mind. He won't kill a mouse that has come into the room. For God's sake, David, they are carriers of disease.' George can hardly contain his frustration. He hops from foot to foot.

But David shakes his head and puts his hand up for my brother to be still. He is crouching down in front of the wardrobe where he and his brother hang their clothes.

'It is probably crawling up your trouser legs and shitting on your things right now,' my brother mutters.

David ignores him. He is listening and making little sucking sounds as if he were calming a hen or a goat. If I hadn't seen it with my own eyes, I wouldn't have believed it, but after a few minutes the mouse comes to him. As soon as David feels the mouse, he picks it up and gently closes his two hands around it.

'Chipo,' he asks very calmly, 'can you bring me a tin or a plastic bag, please?'

I hurriedly unpack the tea and mealie meal I have bought and bring him the bag. Very gently, David lowers the mouse into it. Immediately the mouse begins to panic and scramble. Then it stops and is completely still. It is playing dead.

'I will take it down and let it go outside.'

But I tell David I will. Meanwhile my brother is indicating that I am to murder it. But I ignore him and carry the mouse carefully down to the street, releasing it at the edge of the Company's Gardens behind President's Heights and the derelict car park, where there is, I imagine, plenty of food and good dark holes where it might hide.

When I get home, I find George on his way out. He is furious.

'Everyone in this fucking building is completely mad!' he raves as he pulls on his denim jacket with its Manchester United badge. 'Rat lovers! What next?' He slams the door behind him.

David is sitting by himself at the table, sipping a glass of ginger beer.

'Thank you, Chipo.'

The sunlight is streaming in from behind him. I cannot see his features clearly as I take his repaired trousers from my bag. I have been waiting for a private moment to return them. I feel myself blush. But David pretends not to notice. He examines them, clucking and shaking his head with pleasure at the excellent job Jean-Paul has done. He will hug me now, I think. I want to feel his arms around me. Desire rhymes with fire. It ignites a fire that cannot be put out.

Suddenly the door opens.

'Hey, what's wrong with George? He just passed me in the street. He didn't even stop.'

Jeremiah. Immediately, David turns away from me to greet his friend. His smile is for Jeremiah now.

'Oh, he has things on his mind. It is nothing personal. It's good to see you, Jeremiah. Sit down.'

The hug. Our private moment. Everything evaporates.

Jeremiah sits on a plastic chair. His expression says that he most certainly *does* take it personally. Meanwhile, David hangs up the trousers and goes to the fridge. He doesn't offer Jeremiah a beer because he knows Jeremiah does not drink. Instead he takes out another bottle of Stoney. He pours them each a glass. In his eagerness to fill his friend's glass to the brim, David over-pours and some of the white foam spills over the top.

'Agh, I'm sorry.' David apologises and takes Jeremiah's glass for himself. 'Chipo?' I shake my head. I think that I might cry so I tell them I must get on with preparing dinner. I go to the sink and start to peel the potatoes furiously, dropping each peeled potato into the purple plastic bowl.

'Have you heard? A public holiday for next week's team draw.' Greedily, Jeremiah swallows his remaining ginger beer in two mouthfuls.

'Yes, excellent news,' David agrees.

'You know what that means?' Jeremiah continues as David hurries to refill his friend's glass. 'Double pay at the restaurant, whether Mr Ross likes it or not.'

Seven

Jeremiah is so very boring. When he talks it starts me snoring.

That is my opinion. But I do not dare share it with David. As far as he is concerned, Jeremiah can do no wrong. When during one visit Jeremiah tells us that he has a second-hand computer that does not work properly, and he intends to take it apart to try and rectify the problem, George rolls his eyes and says he has to meet someone. When Jeremiah isn't around, George has taken to calling him 'Choirboy'.

Jeremiah does not seem to notice George's dislike of him. He keeps on talking. Such practical exercises 'keep his brain ticking over'. It is hard doing the mindless, repetitive work of the restaurant.

'I know what you mean,' confides David. 'It is a challenge getting the sort of intellectual stimulation one was accustomed to at university.'

Jeremiah nods. He adjusts the jersey that he has tied over his shoulders. One thing that *can* be said for Jeremiah is that he takes pride in his appearance. He dresses as neatly as a head boy, and he always walks with his head held high, his back straight.

'I love crosswords too. I have a book of crosswords from *The Times* newspaper in the UK. A British woman at the hotel where my mother is working back in Harare gave it to her.'

'But I love crosswords!' exclaims David. 'Really I wanted to study literature rather than law at university.'

Both David and Jeremiah are silent for a moment.

'Well, if you would like,' suggests Jeremiah, 'you could assist me. You know what they say: two heads are better than one.'

David smiles.

I am washing dishes while listening to this conversation. Inside a tiny thorn presses its point into my heart. I rinse a cup under the tap. Why had David never told me that he loved crosswords? Maybe I too could help solve crosswords, if given a chance.

Jeremiah begins to whistle as he pages through the newspaper.

'Oh, look, there is a free concert on at St George's Cathedral. Isn't that just down the road? Let's go. It starts in twenty minutes. We can still make it.'

'Good idea. Chipo, tell Peter that Jeremiah and I have gone out.'

'But dinner is almost ready. I have cooked you samp and beans.'

'Oh, I will eat later, when I get home.'

'But you said you would tell me about your time at university tonight. Your student days.'

'Did I? Well, I can do it tomorrow, can't I? We have to hurry, Chipo.'

'Yes, we don't want to miss the start,' adds Jeremiah.

A half-hour later, Peter arrives home from the bead shop.

'Where is David?' he asks.

'Out with Jeremiah. They have gone to a free concert. Classical music.'

Peter frowns. 'What is he doing, going to listen to that *ngochani* music?'

'*Ngochani* music?' In Shona 'ngochani' means homosexual. I didn't understand what Peter was talking about.

'Never mind, Chipo.'

With a grunt, Peter sits down on his mattress and takes out the key that he keeps on a string around his neck. He pulls the metal chest closer to him. It is in this green chest that he locks away all of his private possessions.

'David is spending too much time with that Jeremiah. I don't like him.'

Is Peter talking to me? I gather up our tin plates and look at him. He has opened his trunk and is putting his wallet inside. I set the plates down on the table and go back for the forks. Does he expect me to answer? Peter closes the lid of his trunk and locks it again. Then he lies down on his mattress and closes his eyes. No. He doesn't expect me to answer. I rinse a glass under the tap and take a drink of water. A fly is on the wall above the sink. Do flies ever get thirsty? They must. Everything, they say, needs water to live.

Don't be angry with David, Chipo, I tell myself as I put the glass down and check the beans to see if they are tender. David has serious responsibilities back home. A whole family and more depend on him and his wages. Peter is always taking care of himself first. That is why David jumps at Jeremiah's offer of a free concert or a book found lying in the street. He is hungry to continue his education, but cannot afford it. Don't hold this against him, even though he has been promising those student-days stories for weeks. Let Choirboy have him tonight. Good to know that Peter doesn't like him either. You'll see. He will make it up to you tomorrow.

But it takes several days, and even then David doesn't exactly apologise.

'Let's go to the science museum.' That is what he says. But I know he is meaning to make it up to me, so I don't pout. Who wants a woman who pouts? I go.

Meg Vandermerwe

The museum of natural history is just around the corner in the Company's Gardens, so George cannot complain. We walk there together. But when we see the cost of entry we change our minds.

'We can go to the government art gallery instead. That's for free for under-eighteens, so at least you won't have to pay, Chipo.'

We walk through the Gardens. It is a quiet place. A place for respite in the middle of the city, with pedestrian paths, patches of green lawn and tall avenues of trees that create lovely places to sit or stroll. I have my umbrella with me but David makes sure we keep to the shady path beneath the trees. We walk past a man in a suit sitting on one of the benches. He is sharing his lunch with a squirrel. The man waits for the creature to stand on its hind legs before he tosses it a corner of his sandwich.

'Agh,' David says under his breath as we pass. 'Just give it the food. Don't make it beg.'

If the man has heard David, he doesn't show it. His cellphone rings and he answers it with a cheery '*Yebo?*'

I have never been to an art gallery before. As we approach it, I catch my breath. It is a large, old-fashioned building painted white, with brown steps leading up to it. Back in Zim such a building would be reserved for politics. Only the wealthy would be allowed to enter it. It wouldn't be an art gallery that just anyone could enter.

I feel a little shy as we push open the heavy glass doors. Even though David has told me that it is open to all, a part of me is scared I might be turned away.

But the woman behind the desk looks right through us as David pays. We pass her and enter the first room, with its ceiling as high as, I imagine, the president's palace back in Harare. It is quiet, neat and bright with white light. My eyes begin to water.

There is a special exhibition on at the moment called 'From Pierneef to Gugu what-what', David says. But David says he hasn't brought me here to see that exhibition. We walk straight through the first room with its paintings and photographs until we enter a second, smaller one. I prefer it. It is dark, and we are the only people apart from the guards in their black blazers.

'Look up,' David says. 'Above that doorway.'

He is pointing to a carved wooden panel that shows seven baboons.

'Look at the one on the far right,' David tells me.

I look. I am grateful for the soft light. I do not want David to see me squinting up like some old woman. 'I see,' I tell him. On the shoulder of the baboon on the far right of the panel is a baby baboon.

'Mother and child,' David says with a smile.

For a moment he turns and looks at me. 'I thought you would like it, Chipo.'

I nod. I do.

'Now I want to show you my favourite.'

We go into the next room. It is even smaller than the one we have just been in. No larger than a very large cupboard. There are two large brown doors with brass fittings that lead, I imagine, to a room piled high with paintings. A room for storing paintings maybe, the way a library stores books. Once again David is not interested in the artwork that is on display. He wants us to look at another wooden panel which he says is forgotten because it sits above the door like a part of the building.

This panel is very different from the previous one. Now there are eleven figures, not seven, and they are not baboons but men. Some of the men are clearly slaves or servants. They are dressed in rags and are on their knees or bent over working the ground. Around them are men who are better dressed, standing tall, barking orders.

'I know what you are wondering. What is so special about that, right? I asked Jeremiah the same question when he showed it to me.'

Choirboy again. David has changed since he and Jeremiah became friends. Not just how he dresses. He hardly drinks any more too, and he has started to use words and phrases that Jeremiah uses, like 'in my humble opinion'. But Jeremiah is not humble. When someone else speaks, he hardly listens.

'Look closely, Chipo.' David says. 'Look at the men's faces.'

I look but I cannot see what all the fuss is about.

'In my humble opinion, whoever made this carving, and it must be very old, has made both the servants and the masters African. You see? The man on the far left.'

David is right. The man on the far left, the one in proper clothes with a hat who is pointing his finger and ordering the slaves about. He is an African too.

We both stand in silence looking at the carving for a few more minutes.

'Come, Chipo,' David says finally. 'We should go.'

Rent day. Peter is sitting at the table counting the piles of brown, pink and blue notes. I come in from washing the laundry in the bath, make myself a cup of tea, take a Tennis biscuit and sit down on my mattress.

My hands smell of Omo and my skin is red and irritated. When there is money I must ask George to buy me a pair of rubber gloves. I sip the tea. It is too hot and makes the tip of my tongue tingle. Peter says nothing.

'Where are the others?' I ask.

'Dublin Bar. Manchester United match.'

Since George is now getting proper wages, Peter says it is only fair if we split the rent fifty-fifty between us. He says this even though George earns less than David, who is a waiter, and Peter makes good money at the bead shop. Still, George doesn't argue. I think he feels fortunate that Peter and David have taken us in and helped us find our feet, even if once they were his homeboys who ate *sadza* cooked by Mama in our house.

From the mattress I watch Peter count.

'Who is playing against Manchester?'

But Peter makes no reply. Counting rent money is a serious business. Each month Peter takes charge of collecting and delivering the money to the landlord. It would be easier if we had a bank account, Peter says. Then we could just make a transfer directly into the landlord's account. But immigrants without ID numbers can't open bank accounts, so Peter has to go and deliver the money personally.

When George gave Peter our share, he first took his time counting the notes to make sure he had been given the correct amount. I think Peter likes to feel the money in his hands. He was the same when he was a boy. Some say that he charged the other children to ride his bicycle only because he liked to count the coins afterwards and feel the weight in his pocket. Peter is not a spender. If he could, I think he would count his money every day and look at it in its piles, the way David looks at books and that wooden panel with the African masters.

'What are you saving for?' George asked him the other night.

'I didn't come to this country to grow old and die here. When I have saved enough, I plan to go home and start a business that will make me rich.'

'What sort of business is that?' George asked. His curiosity was aroused.

'Monkey business,' David piped up, but Peter ignored him.

'You can laugh, brother. Look at you, your nose is always in a book, but where has it got you? When I go home I am going to open a security company. Everyone is worried about their security these days.'

'Well, so long as you are not the one who defends the property.' David and George both laughed. Even as a boy, Peter was known for not being the bravest.

'Laugh all you like. But when you come to me asking for jobs, I will make you beg.'

I watch Peter stuff our share of the rent into the envelope. Soon he will go and knock on Jean-Paul's door. When it comes to the rent, he always addresses Jean-Paul very respectfully, calling him 'Father', as if he is scared that Jean-Paul will realise that he pays more as one person than we do as four.

David is busy with a crossword puzzle, a second-hand dictionary and a pencil at his side. His fingers are long, nimble. His hands, beautiful. There was a book this morning in the window of a bookshop on Long Street: *How to Land Mr Right*.

Land rhymes with hand. Hand rhymes with…

'Tortoise! My jeans?'

I look up from my ironing. George is standing in his underpants with his hands on his hips.

'What is taking so long?'

Today is 20 November, the day before the World Cup team draw. We have been in Cape Town almost two months.

'A hundred and eighty days until the World Cup starts!' Peter announced last night.

'Everyone who is anyone is in Cape Town for this very important occasion,' continues Peter now, reading from the morning paper. World-famous pop stars, famous actresses. Also the South African president. But, most importantly, the paper also says David Beckham is attending.

'The real Beckham?' I ask. 'In the flesh?' The iron spits a cloud of steam as I finish the final seam of George's jeans.

'No, his ghost... Of course the real Beckham.'

'There is a street called Beckham. Off Kloof Street. Near the Spar. I saw it last week.'

My brother nods. He is in a better mood today. Only in South Africa can we have such opportunities, he says. Also, George has a date with his new girlfriend. I think she is called Harmony. Is she Zimbabwean like us, or a South African? I do not know. Back in Beitbridge it was the same. Little Sister's job is to cook and clean, not to stick her nose where it does not belong.

But I *do* know what she looks like. She has beautiful long, braided black hair and skin the colour of coffee with condensed milk in it. I saw her standing with George in the street below while I was washing the windows. I saw her arms around his neck and his around her waist and their bodies pulled tightly together, like the dough of two bread loaves that have run together in the oven. George whistles to himself as he rubs his face with a damp cloth, which he passes back to me in exchange for his jeans.

My brother pulls his jeans on hurriedly when Jean-Paul enters without so much as knocking first. Peter and David are dressed up, too. David in the trousers I had repaired and a pale blue shirt I had ironed for him that morning. He is sucking the pencil now. He looks handsome enough to be the real Andy Cole.

Jean-Paul raises an eyebrow at my brother, who frowns. I do not know why, but these two seem to have taken an instant dislike to each other. Jean-Paul ignores my brother and turns to me.

'Why are you still wearing beige?'

My brother opens his mouth to speak but Jean-Paul puts up his hand to silence him. Miraculously, my brother obeys.

'I only have three dresses, Va Jean-Paul,' I whisper. I can feel my face turning red with shame.

Jean-Paul frowns. 'Well, this is for you.'

A parcel.

'Hey, she had no right to commission something from you. We cannot afford it!'

'It's for free.'

'We are not a charity, you know...'

'Oh, come on, George, at least let her open it.' David coming to my rescue. He closes the book and stands up.

I squeeze the package to my chest.

'Well, go and try it on, Chipo. I haven't got all day.'

In the bathroom I kick off my skirt, whose elastic waistband had long ago grown slack. I cannot remember when I last got new clothes. Not since Mama was alive, that is for sure.

Very carefully, I pull open the tissue paper. Two skirts. Brand new! One red and one green with a yellow pattern. I put on the red one and look down. It fits perfectly. How do I look? Like the sort of woman who could pull off red? I jump to try to catch my reflection in the mirror above the sink, but it is no use.

When I come out, they are all looking at me. But I am watching David.

'Very nice, Chipo.' Without thinking, I throw my arms around

Va Jean-Paul's neck.

'Oh, thank you. They are so beautiful.' Immediately, I feel Jean-Paul's body go rigid. He leans heavily on his cane. I let go. But then, very gently, like I had long imagined a father or uncle would do, he pats my back.

'That's all right, my child,' he whispers, 'that's all right.'

I would have agreed to work for Jean-Paul without wages, but George would never have allowed it.

'He is strange,' protested George.

But when that evening Jean-Paul offered me a hundred rand a week to act as his assistant, saying, 'I have a bad foot. It is not so easy for me to run errands,' my brother immediately agreed.

Within a short time, I learnt that when Jean-Paul is in a good mood, he is full of energy. He can complete as many as two dresses on such days. From deep inside his room, I hear him call, 'More coffee, Chipo!'

Jean-Paul will not drink Nescafé coffee, the one that comes in the glass jar with the gold foil that you must break with a spoon. Poisonous chemicals, he says. It must be coffee made from real beans. He sends me down Long Street to buy it from a shop that sells only coffee beans. It is the first time I have gone so far without my brother. I am told to ask for the Rwandan blend. It costs an enormous hundred and seventy-five rands for one precious kilo. I carry the silver packet back, past the thin coloured youngsters begging tourists to buy them cigarettes and samoosas.

When Jean-Paul shows me how to grind the beans using a small electric machine that growls when you press its lid down, I watch carefully until I am certain I know what to do. Afterwards, his room smells of coffee. This he drinks black with one teaspoon of sugar in it.

'In my country, coffee grows in peoples' back gardens. The landscape is green as far as the eye can see.'

But Jean-Paul's mood is as changeable as Cape Town's weather. It can transform to overcast faster than it takes the rain clouds to sneak over Table Mountain. Sometimes when I knock on his door in the morning he sends me away. He is seeing no one, he says. Helping no one. His voice, from behind the locked door, sounds like he is hissing at me from under his blanket. Sometimes he continues with this puzzling mood for two days. Regardless, he always pays me my one hundred ZARs on Fridays. Extra if I work Saturdays. Other days the door is open, the curtains are back and he sends me down to Adderley Street to buy pink roses or sunflowers or the last of the season's daffodils from the old Malay flower seller whose skin is the colour of cinnamon. She sits on a crate under a blue beach umbrella and eats packets of cheese Nik-Naks.

The first customer he sent me to on the day of the World Cup draw was a family on the first floor. Ugandans. The husband opened the door. He was wearing steel-rimmed glasses like a schoolteacher, and took the parcel without a word. Their flat smelt of cooked bananas.

Meanwhile, outside, Long Street was totally jammed. Thousands had turned out to enjoy the free festivities. A parade of beauty queens from the four corners of the globe. The crowd pressing as close to the stage as it could. Everyone wanted to have a closer look. But not me. Let them have the stage all to themselves while I rely on my imagination to carry me above it all and turn sounds into faces. I felt happy. Maybe George is right, I told myself, lying on our mattress looking up at a great crack in the ceiling plaster later that evening. The others were out, enjoying the celebrations, but I didn't mind. Maybe we have come to the right place just in time. In time for the World Cup, sure. But also for Jean-Paul. For David. Promised Land rhymes with helping hand. I am Jean-Paul's helping hand. And David is mine.

Eight

'Do you ever think about home?'

'Hmmm?'

David looks up from his book, but his eyes show his mind is elsewhere, and he stares straight through me.

'I think about home sometimes,' I continue. 'You know, it is what's familiar. But I do prefer—'

'Sorry, Chipo, I am reading. Can we talk about this later?'

'Oh. No problem.'

I stand up. There is not much for me to do. I have already done the washing and hung it out to dry. Peter and George are on day shift. Jean-Paul's door is closed; he does not want his assistant today. So I go to the window. Down below, the city is busy as usual. Everyone moving, trying to earn their rand.

During the day, Long Street has a different face from the night. It reminds me of the men who would come to Mama's tavern. All respectable at first, but as afternoon turned to evening and evening to night, and the Seven Days brew hit the spot, their shirts would come loose from their trousers, their mouths would hang open and they would start their bedroom talk.

'Bedroom talk' is what Mama called chatter that is best left to the privacy of the bedroom. The sort a man should reserve for his wife and then only when no one else is in earshot. A few litres of Seven Days, though, and it all comes out. Long-seething gripes. Sugary sex talk. Maybe that's why Mama herself never drank. It was only ever cool drinks for her – Coca-Cola, or sometimes a can of green Creme Soda, or, if it was cold, a mug of tea with two teaspoons of sugar dissolved in it that I brought to her from the house. Seven Days makes a man's tongue too loose, Mama said.

'Their secrets creep from their cupboards. If you ever want to see a man's true nature, Chipo, give him a litre of Seven Days and pay attention to what raises its head.'

Mama was right. I saw it often enough. At first, the man would become playful, like a monkey. He is the jester. Wants to win a laugh from everyone. But then two, three litres later, he is an adder. Ready to strike whoever comes too close.

Once, a man on our street was bitten by an adder. It got him in his house. They carried him out by his arms and legs. He was purple, his lips and eyelids swollen. He was dead before anything could be done. People were saying his wife had gone to the *nganga* to arrange that. That he was a husband who drank too much and beat his wife and children when drunk.

Mama poured salt around our doorway. Salt, she said, makes a snake's skin dry out, so they won't slither inside.

'You know what snakes love to eat?' George asked when Mama was out of earshot. 'Albinos.'

'Ha, I have heard that they like small boys. Especially those that like to play soccer!'

George and I made a good game of betting who would be bitten by the snake next. But no one else was bitten.

I want to ask David if he ever saw a man bitten by a snake. But I don't.

～

Christmas sounds like Getting Down to Business. It was always a special festival in our house. Mama would send George and I to buy a chicken from the market. She would slaughter and we would pluck. Chicken, cabbage salad and rice. That was our Christmas feast each year.

'Don't walk next to me. You look like a leper.'

George was referring to the sun cream that Mama had smeared all over me. My brother had recently heard the story of Christ healing the lepers, with their snowy skin. Now he had taken to calling me a leper at every opportunity.

I stood a few metres away as George made the purchase in the bustling market. Even though it was him and not me who they interacted with, the market women still dropped the coins into his hand without touching him.

'Come on, burden.'

Now, David has burdens of his own. With Christmas just two weeks away, this morning I watch him pack a parcel for home. Carefully he arranges the gifts in neat piles on his bed. Four white school shirts. Short-sleeved. Four packets of HB school pencils. Two scientific calculators. Two school rucksacks with front zip pockets. David examines the long list of school supplies that his sister in Harare emailed him on behalf of her two sons. The parcel will have to leave this morning or, by the latest, next Monday if there is to be any hope of it arriving in time for the start of the new school year.

Five minutes. He arrived just five minutes before Peter and so carries all the burdens and responsibilities of the eldest. But what is five minutes? I want to ask him. Why should *you* shoulder such responsibilities while Peter saves his money for who knows what? David never complains, but he sighs as he ticks off the items on the list with a pencil. As well as school supplies, the parcel contains items for the rest of his family: sanitary pads and tampons, perfume as a gift for Margaret, some arthritis medication for his mother and a book about African birds for his father. David was working extra hours at the restaurant to earn the money to cover all the costs. He rubs his eyes and sighs again, louder than the first time, as he ticks the final items off his list.

'Thank God, that's all of it.'

People who like to study birds are called 'ornithologists', David tells me one afternoon. Ornithology sounds like apology. Which is what David's family should give him for placing such responsibilities on his shoulders. Somehow he must still find the money to pay for the *malayitsha* to deliver his precious parcel personally to his family in Harare.

I suppose George and I were fortunate not to have such obligations. Our close family had made it clear, time and time again, that we were an embarrassment. What, an albino for a child *and* a husband who abandoned the family for a tuck-shop owner in Harare? They shook their heads at gatherings and muttered under their breath when we saw them in the street or at the market. Though this sense of shame had not stopped them from knocking on our mother's door when times were still good for her and our tavern was flourishing. Could she lend them a little something until payday? Or could she make a contribution to such-and-such a funeral? Aunt Esther's eldest daughter was getting married and the family needed help to finance the event. How about a contribution? Our mother always obliged, even though as George grew older he grew more and more resentful.

'Why do you help them when they have done nothing for us?' he would reproach her.

Mama would quote from the Bible: 'A generous man will prosper; he who refreshes others will himself be refreshed.'

'But Mama…'

'Real Christian charity, George, is to give without expecting something in return.'

Mama's words proved prophetic. When she grew ill, the family melted away, like water into parched sand. In our community, the feeling was that when someone was struck down by her disease, a disease that no one dared even to name, it was a sign of promiscuity. So when the begging calls and even SMSes started to come through to George and me in Cape Town during those first three months, George took great delight in refusing or deleting them.

But David was different. I could never imagine him abandoning his family, no matter what. He and his older sister Margaret were always particularly close. As I watch David tie string around his bag and knot it once, twice, I think of Margaret. A churchgoer. Quiet. Head girl in her year. When was the last time I saw Margaret or her parents?

Mama wasn't a regular churchgoer. But almost everyone else in our neighbourhood was, including Mama's five brothers and sisters and their families.

'Why don't we go to church like the other children at school?' I asked Mama once when I was seven.

'Because Jesus Christ is everywhere. Not just in a building on Sundays. And you don't need a pastor to talk to Him.'

Two years later, I found out the hard way the real reason we didn't go.

George had gone to church for the first time a few years earlier. It was Auntie Ruth, Mama's eldest sister, who convinced Mama to send him.

'All the children go to church. Do you want your children to stick out like sore thumbs even more than they already do? Come, send the boy for the blessing of becoming a young adult.'

The blessing of the young adult was a special ceremony that took place at Auntie Ruth's church. When children turned twelve it was the custom for them to be specially blessed by the pastor as a mark of their entry into young adulthood.

I was sick in bed with stomach ache that day. Mama stayed home to care for me, and Auntie Ruth took George. So I wasn't there to see it. But when George came home in his suit, carrying a slice of cake wrapped in a piece of newspaper, he said it was 'all right'.

The morning before we went to church for my blessing, Mama washed me from head to toe and combed my hair down with hair cream. George wanted to shave his head to look like Tupac, but Mama cuffed his ears and told him sharply to put on his school tie and stop his games.

Because we were not members of our own church, we were going to Auntie Ruth's, where a new pastor had recently joined the congregation. I looked in Mama's bedroom mirror as she tied a white ribbon into my hair.

'You look very pretty,' she said and kissed the top of my head.

'Come, George, turn off that television. Today we are churchgoers.'

It seemed to start fine. Not too many looks as we slipped into the three seats next to Auntie Ruth, Uncle John and their three boys. Auntie Ruth's youngest stuck his tongue out at me, but I was used to that. We all rose to sing with the choir. Then sat again to listen to the pastor's sermon, which was all about temptation.

'The Dev-il comes in all guises, my brothers and sisters. Yes, he is a master of temp-ta-tions! Wine and women. Wine that dulls the senses and creates for lax morals. Women who tempt us into siiiin with their charms.'

Mama shifted uncomfortably like she was sitting on a heap of termites, but kept her face calm and her hands folded around the purse in her lap.

The sermon went on for a very long time, and if it wasn't for the pastor's habit of raising his voice at the end of each sentence until his voice boomed, demolishing our private thoughts, I think more men than Uncle John would have nodded off. Poor man. Every time he bowed his head and began to snore, Auntie Ruth would give him a violent elbow jab in the ribs so that his head would pop up like a frightened horse.

Finally, it was time for the children who were to receive their first special blessing to make their way to the front. The middle aisle filled with boys and girls all dressed in white. Some were holding flowers, like brides. Today their souls are marrying Jesus Christ, said Auntie Ruth.

'Go on,' Mama whispered, and she gently nudged me from the seat, 'it will be all right.'

Auntie Ruth was beaming like she had just won the lottery. She was a great believer, and was perhaps hoping that if all went well her wayward sister might become one of the saved.

'Go on, go on.' With a flick of her wrist she encouraged me to join the back of the queue.

On the way to the church, I had heard Mama quiz Auntie Ruth again about the proceedings.

'You are certain he knows the situation?'

'I already told you. He knows everything.'

'But you haven't yet told me what he said.'

'Nothing.'

'Nothing?'

'I have already told you, sister. When I told him about Chipo, he asked about your marriage…'

'What has my marriage got to do with anything?'

'I do not know. But he said Chipo could come. That is the most important thing. He is a good man, Grace. A kind man. Do not worry.'

One. The next. Another. As I edged up the aisle behind the other children I could feel the eyes of all upon me. I turned back to look at Mama, who was watching me anxiously. It was just me left. The other children had returned to their seats. I knelt at the altar and closed my eyes as Mama had told me to do. But no blessing came.

'Stop! Stop stop stop!' the pastor called. I suppose he had been waiting for this moment. The choir fell silent. The congregation held its collective breath.

'Stand up, girl.'

Awkwardly, I got up.

'Stand and face the congregation.'

I did as he commanded. I could see that Mama wanted to rise, but Auntie Ruth was telling her to stay where she was.

'You see this girl? I was visited in a dream…' the pastor began, 'a dream, my friends, and in that dream the message was clear. She bears the mark of the *sope*. It is a curse.'

The congregation gasped, Mama and Auntie Ruth included, but the pastor raised his hands for quiet.

'A curse that signifies the sins of her parents. The curse of the mother shall be visited upon the offspring. As much as Cain's mark branded him as one cursed by God.'

The pastor fell silent for a moment. What was he talking about? I did not know. All I knew was that there would be no blessing for me.

'She must repent and the ancestors be properly appeased. Let us pray together.'

The pastor pushed me down onto my knees. The congregation was still deathly silent. Without a moment's hesitation, Mama stood up. She pushed past her fellow congregants, who sat rigid as useless boulders, and marched to the front. She picked me up and jerked my brother by the arm from his seat before marching us outside.

Back home, my brother was only too happy to be allowed to play with his soccer ball in the street. Mama didn't even make him change out of his suit first. Meanwhile, Mama soothed me, rocking me close as I sobbed. I could smell her Oil of Olay, but its familiar scent offered no comfort.

Do not cry, she told me. They had once done such a thing to a friend of hers, too.

'What friend, Mama?' I sniffed.

'You don't know her. She no longer lives here.'

'Where does she live?'

'Eh, she lives in Porttown, last I heard – do you want to hear the story or not?'

I nodded.

'After two years of marriage she had yet to produce a child. Her husband, a religious man, had insisted that they go and pray for help. In the church every Sunday, this friend, she stood as members of the congregation and the pastor and her husband laid hands on her and spoke in tongues demanding that the demon that was filling her womb with concrete be driven out.'

'Did it work?'

My mother shook her head. 'No. Eventually she refused to go with her husband, who left her, calling her a *mhanje*. That's the word in our culture for the lowest form of womanhood, a barren woman. But there is a happy end to the story. She married again and now has four children, last I heard.'

Mama stood up. 'That pastor is a self-righteous, superstitious idiot. When he talks it is like watching a pot of porridge bubble with hot air. I should never have listened to Auntie Ruth. When he asked about your father, I should have known that he was planning monkey business. Come, no tears. Let's watch that match between Manchester and Tottenham. We will find a new church.' Mama would never return to any church.

But I was angry at her that morning. If she knew that people were like that, how could she have let me go into the viper's nest?

'You must get strong. If you wait for others to do good by you, you will be waiting a long time. Believe me, I know it. Besides, do not think that God isn't watching them and taking account.'

And then, in a softer voice, she told me to go and fetch the bottle of lotion in the bedroom. Undoing the buttons at the back of my dress, she rubbed the lotion into my skin.

As I watch David tying string around the *tshangani* bag, making it ready for collection, I wonder if he still remembers that day, so many years ago? And Margaret? I do not like the thought of David or his sister feeling sorry for me. I go to the window and look out. Below, a white woman is walking with a child and an old *bakkie* is struggling to park while the other motorists hoot.

~

Church or no church, I want our first Christmas in Cape Town to be special, like it used to be with Mama. When it approaches, I decide to make chicken, cabbage salad and rice, just like Mama used to at home. There is plenty to celebrate, I told George a few days earlier. For one thing, it was the first time in four years that we could afford such a meal.

'Ha,' George said, 'so you think we are rich?' But he and the others agreed.

Outside, I can see that the bars and restaurants are making their final preparations for the Christmas festivities too. A girl with spiky pink hair at the Billabong shop is sticking pictures of snowmen and snowflakes in the window, even though Christmas comes at the height of summer here. 'Season's Greetings' is what most of the shop windows say.

When I was at school and we were given Charles Dickens to read, I wondered what it would be like to see and taste snow. Mama had distant cousins who lived in the north of England, in Newcastle. One year they sent us a photograph of them all standing holding lumps of ice in the palms of their hands. In England it snows often, Mama told me. At the time I held the photo under my nose and squinted from the snow to my cousins' amused eyes, back to the snow.

Secretly, I knew that Mama dreamt of one day visiting Great Britain. In particular, I knew it was her wish to make her way to Manchester and see the real Old Trafford, where her favourite team played.

I wish I could have been the one to enable such a visit. I am thinking such thoughts as I make my way into the Mountain Dew Superette.

The Mountain Dew Superette is always dark and cool, even on hot summer days. Superette sounds like we do not sweat. There is never a fan to cool the sweating face of the Somali owner, like in our tin-roofed *spazas* back home. Inside, the Somalis sell tired fruit and vegetables: oranges, apples, onions, potatoes. Packets of Marie and Tennis biscuits. Toilet paper – single ply. Newspapers. Magazines – *You* and *TV Guide*. Bleach for cleaning toilets and sinks. Green Sunlight liquid for washing pots and dishes. Ricoffee. Sugar. Long-life milk. Tea. Because it is open twenty-four hours, there are times you can go there, such as very early in the morning, and guarantee that it will be quiet.

I am here to get ingredients for our Christmas lunch. I buy rice. Cooking oil. Two onions. Two heads of cabbage. For the chicken I will have to walk to the Spar on Kloof Street.

On Christmas Day itself, I wear the red skirt David admires and prepare the meal with great care.

'See,' says George, patting his swollen belly after his first two helpings. 'Life is not so bad here after all. And, what's more, there are only, what, forty-eight weeks until the WC.'

'Don't say WC. It sounds like you are talking about the toilet, not the World Cup,' David jokes.

Peter bursts into laughter and spits out his cabbage.

I have been watching David eat.

'Is it all right?' I ask as he hands me his plate for extra rice.

'Delicious, Chipo, as always.'

'Oooooh, David, you know I always cook so delicious just for you.'

George. I glare at my brother. I do not care what he says. He can do nothing to dampen my mood. With ease and grace I serve David another large spoonful. Today at least I am the proper woman of this house.

After I serve the others, I decide I will take Jean-Paul a plate of food too. His door is closed, so I know to knock before entering. Why is it that he never seems to have any visitors, apart from clients? And why does he never seem to go out? Does he not have someone with whom to spend Christmas?

'Va Jean-Paul?'

No answer. I try again.

'Va Jean-Paul, it is me. I have some Christmas lunch for you. Chicken and rice. It is still warm.'

The door opens. Jean-Paul is wearing a long robe. He looks like a pastor.

'What is it? I am occupied.' I peer into the room. It is empty and dark and smells of sweat and heat. I hold out the plate.

'No, thank you, Chipo. I must go.'

I go back to the table, where the others are still talking and eating. My brother is helping himself to the last scrapings from the pot.

'What's going on with Mr Congo? Too good for our food?'

'He has already eaten,' I lie. I pass the plate to my brother who, using his fork, divides the portion between himself, Peter and David.

'You know, perhaps Jean-Paul is the wisest one. At least he works for himself. He doesn't rely on anyone else for a job.' That is Peter. He has been drinking beer all afternoon since coming home from church and is in a merry mood.

My brother belches. 'Master? Ha! If I was his customer I wouldn't let my backside leave the wall. Have you noticed how he never has a woman? It's not natural.'

Peter nods his agreement and raises his beer bottle to his lips. David says nothing.

'At least you know your sister is safe with him,' says Peter, spooning the last of the food into his mouth. 'And he pays the largest share of the rent,' he reminds the others, his eyes now foggy from alcohol. 'Let us not forget that. Even if he is a Buttock Beak.'

David frowns but Peter laughs and shakes his head.

George looks at me. His eyes struggle to focus. I can see he is drunk too. 'Ha ha. Chipo's friend. A Buttock Beak…'

Peter points his hand at David as though it is a gun and takes aim. 'You hear that, brother? Buttock Beak, bang bang!'

There is a woman. Every morning I watch her from the window. She leaves President's Heights at six-thirty and returns again in the evening, sometimes as late as eight. Sometimes she is carrying a small blue plastic bag from the Mountain Dew Superette. Sometimes not. Sometimes she carries a faded black umbrella, sometimes not. She always wears a black cardigan. Her skin is dark. Very dark. I do not think she is from Zimbabwe. Is she from the Democratic Republic of the Congo, like Jean-Paul? Or Cameroon? Nigeria? Could even be Mozambique. She looks George's age, or perhaps a few years older. Over her shoulder a black handbag hangs limply. It looks empty. No matter what the weather, this woman walks with her shoulders hunched. It looks like she is always cold. Is she cold? Why is this woman always alone?

Every day I watch her while I wait for the water to boil for George's tea and again when I am washing up after preparing dinner. She does not know that I am watching her. I know that we will probably never meet, but I want to ask her, 'What's your name?' and 'Where do you come from?'

Nine

'Turn.' Jean-Paul circles around me. 'These Somali boys are so thin. Don't fidget, please, Chipo. Don't know what their mothers and grandmothers feed them. Mussolini's spaghetti.'

He laughs, and then stops abruptly, as if laughter were a sin.

I am wearing a blazer Jean-Paul has been given to alter in time for the start of the new secondary-school year in January, in three days' time. I was there when the mother arrived. Mrs Shire, wife of Mohammed, the manager of the Mountain Dew Superette, wearing her black hijab. Her son had got into Gardens Commercial High School. This apparently is something to celebrate, as not just anyone can get in, even though it is a government school. You have to be good at science or maths. Her son stood looking embarrassed as his mother continued her boasting. 'Sleeves too long,' she said. She had bought it second-hand. 'You fix.'

Jean-Paul nods to indicate I am to take the blazer off. It is ready to be delivered.

'Jean-Paul, is it true about the man who starved to death waiting for his asylum papers?' I do not want to make my new friend uncomfortable, but I had not been able to get the image of that poor man out of my head these past months, and I did not know who else to ask.

Jean-Paul takes the pins from his mouth and slowly puts them back in their tin. He sighs.

'It is. He used to live right here in President's Heights...'

I had already heard this from Peter and David.

'Do you believe in *fantômes*, Chipo?'

'*Fantômes*?'

Jean-Paul hangs the blazer on a wire hanger. 'You know, the spirits of the dead. The ones that won't go away.'

'Oh, a ghost.'

'Yes yes, a ghost. They say his ghost still haunts this place. I can believe it. You see, it does not know what to do. It died far from home and its own people. It is a *fantôme* caught between home and here, between this world and the next. Very bad.'

Very bad. This, I will learn, is what Jean-Paul says when a story is too terrible to tell. Very very bad. Bad. Sad. Mad.

'And he is not the only one, you know. Not the only ghost we have living here.' Jean-Paul glances in the direction of the photograph. 'Still, at least his family know where he is. It is worse not to. Not to know.'

I look at the photograph too. Today there is a new bunch of pink roses next to it, and two statues of the Virgin Mary stand guard on either side.

I want to ask Jean-Paul about the woman and child in the photograph. I do not yet possess the courage. Who are they? His wife and daughter? Why aren't they here with him? When was the photo taken? I know that Jean-Paul sees me looking, but he pretends not to.

'Take this blazer downstairs, Chipo. Mr Mohammed is expecting it. And please bring me back one orange.'

~

Making clothing takes time and effort. But it can make a big difference to people's lives. That is what Jean-Paul tells me. He always injects some of the personality of his clients into the items. That is why his customers are so satisfied.

'For example, that lady who came last week, Chipo. The one with the scar here…' Jean-Paul points to his cheek.

I nod. I know the one.

'I saw, in spite of her serious appearance, she has a lighter character. Meaning she is more joyful. So I included a bow on each sleeve. She did not ask me for one, but when she saw it, was she not thrilled?'

It is true. She was. I nod again. When Jean-Paul says 'thrilled', it sounds like 'trilled'. He hardly ever pronounces his h's. Must be how people speak English in the Congo, I tell myself.

'You know those young men who always look like they are going to a wedding? The ones from DRC?'

'David says they refuse to dress like poor men.'

'True. Back in Congo they are called *sapeurs*. Know why?'

I shake my head.

'They are men who worship the cloth. And I don't mean the holy cloth. For them the fashion cloth is what's holy. Am I making sense?'

He isn't making much sense to me. But I have learnt that when he chatters this way, not giving me a moment to speak, that the best thing to do is smile and nod. Jean-Paul continues.

'What you wear affects how you feel. You may be a poor man, but when you dress like a rich one, like a successful one, it changes everything. It gives you room to dream. To hope.'

'So how do you do this?' I ask Jean-Paul.

'I can read something of their soul. For example, a woman comes here. She is working for a white lady, cleaning her house. But she dreams of being a nurse. I help to make her look like a nurse, meaning a professional who is respected. So at least on Sundays at church, she is closer to her dream. She looks in the mirror and that is what she sees.'

Working for Jean-Paul has made me more conscious of what I wear, too. Every day I make sure my blouse is clean and pressed. As I look in the mirror that night, I wonder to myself, what would the wife of David look like? She would look respectable. Would she be fashionable? I look in the mirror and stare hard. Examine. Imagine. She would not be a tin of condensed milk like me. She would have beautiful dark skin. She would definitely have long dark hair, too. There is nothing you can do to change your skin, Chipo, I tell my reflection that night, but you can try to do something about this hair of yours.

I am thirteen. I am watching young lovers. I know they are lovers because they look into each other's eyes and speak with their faces so close that their words pass into each other's mouths. That is the way Mama and Stanley used to look at each other. The tongues. I cannot look away. The smiling woman pushes her nose into her lover's neck. He pulls her closer.

That night I go home and beneath the bedcovers I run my hands over my adolescent breasts. Immediately my nipples harden. My lover is above me. Dark. Handsome. He is leaning over me. He is pushing his tongue inside my mouth. He is speaking his words into me the way Mama says God once breathed his voice into clay to make human flesh.

~

I have heard that there is a hairdresser in the Pan African Market on Long Street who specialises in African weaves and styles. So I go there the next morning, as soon as I think it might be open.

The Pan African Market is a collection of different shops selling African curios and carvings to tourists. But there are also Africans offering services. As I make my way through the rooms with their walls painted bright red, blue and yellow, out of the shadows step handsome black men, with smiles like slices of sweet melon when they think they can smell foreign currency. Most ignore me when they see that I am not a real white.

'Africa hairdresser's is on the third floor. Last room,' a man making baskets from colourful plastic beads and wire coat hangers tells me, when I ask.

When I reach the room, I find that it is empty except for three large women and one white tourist.

The women are not South African. They are not Zimbabwean. They cluck their tongues and chatter among themselves as the white woman listens to her headphones and flicks through a guidebook with pictures of lions and elephants on the cover.

One woman approaches me: 'Yes, sister?'

'I want what she is having.' I point to a photo from a magazine on the wall of a black woman with beautiful dark braids.

She shakes her head and points to the blonde tourist, whose hair is being plaited.

'No, I want black hair. Like an African.'

The woman shrugs and says something to the two women doing the plaiting. Both laugh. Then she offers me a seat.

'Nearly finish. Please wait.'

Having braids put in takes a long time. Hours. Almost as long as waiting at Home Affairs. After six hours of the two women working feverishly on my head, my scalp feels pinched and bruised, but I am ready. I pay the money that I have begged Jean-Paul to lend me and go.

As I walk up Long Street I catch my reflection and I know that I glow. This is closer to what David's bride would look like. Of that I am certain. My heart thumps with pride. And if I look like it, am I not one step closer? Isn't that what Jean-Paul says?

'Chipo, you look so beautiful!'

'Oh, David, you think so? I just thought, you know, a change.'

'But, Chipo, I cannot take my eyes off you. Would you like to go…'

Where would we go? Where would David take his future bride? Not to the Joburg Bar, that's for certain. Not to that greasy-looking café either, I think, as I pass it. Somewhere… grander. The Waterfront. Yes, somewhere at the Waterfront mall. Isn't that where the wealthy go? I can see David and me sitting at a table overlooking the ocean. At our feet are parcels and bags – purchases he has made for me. I sip my cappuccino. He leans forward and, looking into my eyes, takes my hand. We do not need to speak. We have that quality lovers have, who know from a gesture, from a smile, what the other one is thinking.

My body is trembling with excitement as I turn the key in the door. If I were on television, the theme music would start now.

The radio is on. Thumping American hip-hop. The sort that makes the glasses drying next to the sink rattle. So, George is home.

'Tortoise?'

'Yes, George.'

'Where have you been, hey?' he asks, without turning around to look at me.

'Out,' I say. I put down my bag. 'George?' I cannot wait to hear what he says. Chipo. Not Tortoise. Not Little Sister. *Chipo*.

'Ha ha!' My brother bends over with laughter. 'Your hair. You look like a zebra! Peter, Peter, come here! Look what Chipo has done to herself.'

'Shut up, George!' I scream like a madwoman. I tear past Peter, who has stepped out of the toilet, and run to Jean-Paul's room.

Jean-Paul says nothing. He watches me weep on a chair for a few moments. It is true. Looking in Jean-Paul's mirror, I see how ridiculous it looks – the bottom and roots still blonde, the braids black. Jean-Paul pushes a box of tissues in my direction. Then he hands me his tailoring scissors.

When David gets home and George tells him the story, I have already pulled most of the braids out.

I can see him looking at me. He is puzzled. Normally, I am the first to greet him, but I feel so foolish that I cannot look at him. Tonight I want him to ignore me until I am back to my old self.

'Chipo, tell David what you did today.'

I ignore George and continue to comb out my hair.

David shrugs and sits down. Thankfully, George doesn't pursue it. He has another bone to pick.

'I don't know how you can stay at Jeremiah's place. I hate Wynberg Main Road. All those Congolese everywhere, eating their horrible stinking dried fish.'

David raises his eyebrows at George as he spoons some mealie porridge into his bowl.

'What, David? I just don't like how they present themselves as African Rambos, OK? Why must they always be security? I tell you what, they think they are still commandos and we must be waiters. I could beat the shit out of any Congolese, no problem.'

'Sure, George.' David catches my eye and winks. 'Chipo, what are your plans tonight?' he asks.

'I am helping Jean-Paul. I am ironing his alterations.' All the braids are out now. I brush my hair down.

'Could you wash my green shirt?'

'Of course, David.'

'Excellent. I want to wear it tomorrow.'

'Are you going out *again*?' I can't disguise my disappointment.

David nods. 'Yes. Jeremiah says there's a free lunchtime talk on at the university. Oh, damn, I'm going to be late for the restaurant. Mr Ross will rant. Try to stay out of trouble, Rambo. See you later, Chipo.'

When David is gone, my brother turns back to me. 'So Chipo's favourite is out again tomorrow night with Choirboy. Shame.'

Ten

They say that it is when your bread is buttered that you must hold onto it the tightest, because that is when life comes to snatch it away. That is what happened to Mama with Old Trafford.

After four months in Cape Town, we are full of hope. New Year came and went. Yes, we have survived so far, we tell ourselves. George and I have regular jobs. We can keep our heads above water when it comes to buying food and life's necessities. We can meet the rent.

By February, George decides we can even afford a second-hand television. On the day it arrives, David and Peter, but also several of the Zimbabwean waiters with whom George and David work, including Jeremiah, come to admire this new luxury.

'Almost a flatscreen,' announces George proudly, as he adjusts the bent antenna in an attempt to correct the snowy picture. He has bought it from a group of Nigerians downstairs. They are letting him pay it off at one hundred ZARs a month and have included a VCR on loan and some Nollywood films for free.

Nollywood sounds like Hollywood, but it is nothing like Hollywood. Still, these Nigerian films, with their gory shoot-outs, zombie possessions and witch-doctor curses become firm favourites with my brother and his friends, along with the *WWE Raw*,

Isidingo, a show about wealthy black and white South Africans, and of course all the soccer fixtures.

'You see, Jeremiah,' says George one evening as they watch a copy of *Joseph's Twins*, about one twin who was in league with the Devil, 'such films are more than entertainment. Granted, it is not like a game of chess. But we who did not go to university must be satisfied.'

Jeremiah shrugs and says nothing. He snaps a peanut from its shell and offers one to David. They do not care much for the new television, except if the soccer is on. Instead they are hunched over Jeremiah's chessboard, which sits on an old bottle crate.

My brother turns up the volume.

David stares hard at the pieces on the chessboard in front of him. Jeremiah is teaching him how to play, but he has yet to master the game and still makes lots of careless mistakes.

'No, David.' Jeremiah shakes his head. He has told David before: if you lift a piece from the board, place it elsewhere and lift your hand, you cannot change your mind. That is 'chess etiquette'.

Jeremiah is very concerned with etiquette. He does not like it when George swears and farts. He shakes his head and clicks his tongue whenever someone takes the Lord's name in vain.

Embarrassed, David smiles and apologises. He puts the piece back.

'You will get the hang of it,' Jeremiah tells him. 'Practice and discipline. Those are the secrets.' Jeremiah picks up a chess piece and moves it forwards. 'Now watch out, my friend, you have left your queen unprotected.'

Yes, slowly slowly, we seem to be succeeding. But our new home still holds some surprises for us. It starts with a phone call at the end of February that scoops me out of sleep like a fisherman's net. I open my eyes. My cellphone, a gift from Jean-Paul, is glowing, ghostly and impatient. I swallow. I had been having another nightmare. Not Mama. This time the *magumaguma* gangs along the border. They had knives ready to cut out my organs for *muti*. I breathe in, out. Wait for my racing heart to slow. You are safe, Chipo. Safe safe safe. Still groggy, I reach for the phone.

'George?'

'No, it's David. Listen, Chipo, I haven't got much airtime. We are at the police station. George has been arrested.'

Arrested? I repeat the word.

'Arrested?' My mouth is dry.

'Don't worry. He is fine. They are going to release him. We will be home as soon as we can. I just thought you should know...'

Other voices.

'Sorry, Chipo, I have to go.'

Fear is a sharp word. It makes your tongue bleed. Anger is sour and fiery. Like acid indigestion. Hatred. Hatred is a word that gets stuck in your throat. Xenophobia. Xenophobia is a long word. Complicated, arrogant. It thinks it is smarter than other words. It is a bully. Anxiety is a terrible word. It is the ground turning to quicksand beneath you.

When I look back on it now, from here, I can see that there were warning signs of the troubles to come. Our treatment at Home Affairs. That afternoon in December when David came back, furious because a Xhosa-speaking saleslady had refused to speak English to him when he asked for help at a department store in Adderley Street.

'*I reported her to the manager, as if he will do anything.*'

And then there were the unfriendly comments from the Xhosa locals.

'*Hey*, makwerekwere! *Go back to your own country!*'

'*Hey, we know you are only here to take our jobs and money.*'

And of course before. I am talking about the smoke of May 2008. From here I can still see it, although most people cannot. It is a stain that cannot be washed out. That smoke spread like blood over the houses of those foreigners burned out of the townships by their African brothers and sisters who bared their teeth and raised their pangas, chanting, 'Go home or die here!'

Refugees rhymes with fleas. And fleas must have their heads squeezed off.

And yes, word reached us back in Zimbabwe. Sixty killed. One hundred thousand displaced. One Zimbabwean man in Joburg was burnt alive. Petrol poured on his body and matches thrown until he ran and rolled himself on the ground like a fallen star. Criminal elements, not locals, is what the South African newspapers said. Our government newspapers back home paraded the stories, as if to say: 'So you want a better life across the border? Ha!'

But there is a saying, that hope springs eternal. Back in Zimbabwe, before we left, George dismissed any possibility of encountering such troubles: 'There is xenophobia everywhere. Even here. Besides, that was long ago. South Africa says they will host the World Cup on behalf of all Africa. Does that sound like a country that plans to turn on its African brothers and sisters?'

After George's arrest we are confused and frightened. The most upset of all is Jeremiah. He begins to tremble when George recounts the story of how he and Harmony were assaulted by a ticket inspector on a train and then arrested even though they had been the innocent party.

'He attacked you because he thought she was a local girl. That you were stealing their women. You know how they all talk about us taking their South African girls.' That is Peter's view on the attack.

But it isn't the attack alone that is causing a commotion among us. It is what the ticket inspector said: 'Just you wait. When the World Cup is finished, we will drive all you foreigners out! If you stay, you will burn!'

'He was drunk,' David soothes.

'He meant it! And not one of those police bastards did a thing! They arrested us and let him go. It is just like back home, except here they do not abuse you because you are poor, but because you are poor and a foreigner. South Africa welcomes the world, my shit!' George spits out the official catch phrase for the World Cup.

'The more I am here, the more I wonder if we are not better off back home.' This is Jeremiah.

'Ha! Back home we'll starve!' Peter is losing his temper.

'And here? Here we'll burn!'

Jeremiah. David looks very concerned about his friend. For a moment he looks like he might reach out and touch him, but then he seems to think better of it. Jeremiah has his reasons to worry, David says, after Jeremiah has gone. He fetches himself a Castle from the fridge, even though David usually only drinks on weekends.

David opens the bottle and drinks deeply. I can see that he too is rattled, although he is trying his best not to show it.

'Jeremiah never told you what happened to his cousin in 2008.'

He takes another swig.

'His cousin was a young man like him – strong. But one day he complained of a terrible fever and headache. It was just before all the troubles in May. Jeremiah took him to the hospital near the Waterfront. But those people would not help him…'

'Who?' my brother asks, tenderly massaging Zam-Buk into his swollen jaw where the inspector punched him.

'The nurses. They asked Jeremiah's cousin for his name and family name so they could fill in their forms. When he told them the nurse replied, "But that is not a Xhosa name. You cannot be from here." Immediately she left. And each time Jeremiah went to find her, she and her colleagues pretended to be too busy to help.

'After eight hours of waiting and no help, Jeremiah and his friends brought the young man back here, and during the night he died. Jeremiah used all the money he had saved to bring his wife and daughter to South Africa, to store the body in the morgue and get him a proper burial.'

David shakes his head and slumps down into a chair. Peter just sits stock-still. George snorts and lights a cigarette. They will both have to leave for work in an hour and have yet to get some sleep.

Eleven

Saturday morning. Early March. Five months since George and I arrived in Cape Town. A hundred and twenty-five days until the World Cup kick-off. None of us has been the same since the night of George's attack. Now, waiting for the World Cup doesn't fill us with excitement. It fills us with trepidation. It seems the threats spat at George by the ticket inspector have begun to be heard by others.

'Let's go to the internet café,' David says. He will teach me about Google Earth.

Together we walk to the café on the corner. It is the cheapest, set up in a corridor of a building and costing just five rand for thirty minutes. We pay our money and sit at a monitor.

'It works by satellite. See, if you zoom you can see the exact spot in Beitbridge where your house is.'

'Was.'

'Sorry, was. But still, isn't it incredible, Chipo? Jeremiah has taught me all about it. Look, there's our old school. And there is the tree where Peter was chased by the vice-principal for kicking a soccer ball at his head. Do you remember?'

And Mama's grave? But I do not ask to see that. Instead I tell David that I want to see the Old Trafford soccer ground in Manchester.

'Can we?'

'Just watch.'

A few clicks on the keyboard and mouse. There it is. The pitch and buildings I know our mother would have given anything to visit. David and I wait for the image to grow clear and solid. It looks very small.

'One day, I will take you to the real Old Trafford, my children. We will walk where the greatest red shirts have.' This memory of Mama's promise, as I helped her to stir the Seven Days fermenting in buckets, one happy evening, long before our troubles started, comes to me as I watch David trying to enlarge the image further.

'Look, you can see the stands and individual seats!'

Over the next month, for five rand a half-hour, David and I 'visit' the original Old Trafford many times. Also New York's Statue of Liberty. Paris and the Eiffel Tower, London and Buckingham Place. David says it is like looking through 'God's spectacles'.

'Imagine if they can create a computer programme that allows you to see into the future,' David says. 'I suppose the American military will like that. It is they who developed this technology, you know. For spying and what-what. It would be good, too, to know if we are to take these xenophobic rumours seriously.'

Imagine, I repeat. Imagine if one can look into the future. Not just of countries. But into our own futures too.

'Have you ever been to the townships?'

'No, never.'

'George says that the people who want us to leave live there. He says that he cannot believe it. We are all Africans, and yet they see us as worse than colonisers.'

I watch Jean-Paul carefully measure the fabric. He marks it with his tailor's chalk and then cuts it, piece by piece, shape by shape. I think he is making a jacket. So far he has shown no emotion. Has he heard the rumour? Does he not care?

'Jean-Paul, they say we have until the World Cup final to leave. We can stay until then but after that they will drive us back across the borders.'

'Where did George hear that?'

'From the ticket inspector who attacked him.' I pass Jean-Paul the pins. 'But also at the restaurant. From the waiters who take the train in from Observatory. Complete strangers have started approaching them. They say, "We are giving you until the World Cup final. After that, you better go home." And it's not just on the trains. Peter's girlfriend, Aneni, says that a Xhosa woman, a woman at the hotel where she cleans, said to her, "Sorry for you. When the World Cup is finished, you will burn."'

Still Jean-Paul shows no emotion. Does he not believe me?

'George says we are probably safe in the city, though. That it is the foreigners living and working in the locations who must worry. A lot of Somalis have tuck shops there, apparently. Here we are among our own. Is that why we don't live in the locations but in town? To be among our own?'

'Perhaps. But I live in town because that is where my clients are.'

I think about Luthumba, Beitbridge's location. It stood a few minutes outside the town centre. I wonder about Cape Town's locations. Khayelitsha. Gugulethu. Nyanga. They don't sound or rhyme like anything. What are they like? Their homes? Their schools? Markets? Soccer pitches? Surely the same as ours?

Mama once told me a story about when she was a girl.

'There was a bad drought. Not a drop of rain for almost three years, *mwanangu*. Things became scarcer and scarcer. First fresh goods, fruit and whatnot. Then meat. The women started to fight at the markets and in the shops for mealie meal, for samp and rice. Neighbour versus neighbour. Sister versus sister. Mothers against daughters.'

I told Jean-Paul the story. He shook his head. But there was no drought here. Wasn't there enough for everyone, even us foreigners? Jean-Paul did not look at me. He carefully pinned the front and back pieces of fabric together. I was growing frustrated by his silence.

'When we are scared for our livelihoods, we can do terrible things,' he replied finally.

'Were you here the last time? In 2008?'

'Yes.'

'So what do we do?'

'We wait.'

I want to talk to Jean-Paul about this, but I can see he is in no mood to discuss such matters. He works silently, his forehead creased into a frown. I pull a chair to the window and sit down.

Below in the street, how many were visitors? Tourists or those just passing through Cape Town? Foreigners like us, yet everyone greets them with open arms because they have money.

Rent day. It always puts George in a foul mood. He says he would rather be hanging on to his hard-earned wages than giving them away to fat-bellied South African strangers. But Peter is strict. The rent is not allowed to be late. Late rent means there is a good chance we will be put out onto the street.

Today George is in an even worse mood than normal when he hands over the blue and pink notes. He says that last night Mr

Ross made him clean human shit off the pavement in front of the restaurant. He says he has had enough of Mr Ross's orders, and something more lucrative must come soon.

'If the stinking manure does fall from the cart in July, I don't want to have made this journey for nothing.'

Everyone has been talking about the new rumours. They seem to have infiltrated every community – the Zimbabweans, the Congolese, the Cameroonians, Malawians, Nigerians, Somalis. Before, we looked forward to the arrival of the World Cup. It was something to be celebrated. But we no longer trust it. Still, no one is talking about leaving South Africa yet. I think they are hoping to get a slice of all the tourist cash that everyone has been promised. George, too, is hoping to profit.

'Maybe their money will be the answer to all our troubles,' he told Peter and David last week. 'We will make enough money to go home and live easy for a while.'

Then one evening George comes home with more bad news. Luc from the restaurant has gone.

Luc's job was to stand outside Tortilla and stop the street children from putting the tourists off their refried beans and beer.

'But on Monday he didn't turn up for work.'

Three nights passed and still no Luc. He wasn't answering his cellphone either, says George. Mr Ross ranted a lot. He said Luc had better stay away because as soon as he stepped through the door, he would fire his black backside anyway.

'But word has come from Luc's cousin today. He's been refused his residence permit. When he went to Home Affairs to get his six-month update, they arrested him on the spot. This is how they are now doing it. Art of surprise. They are putting us in prison until the deportation plane leaves. A normal prison with common criminals. That way, they are sure to wash the taste for South Africa from our mouths.' George sits down and lights a cigarette.

'But Luc has a wife and two children in South Africa,' David replies. 'His wife's decision is still pending, but he is on a plane back to the Congo. So now their family is split apart?'

George nods.

David's forehead is creased like a shirt in need of ironing. Jean-Paul is from the DRC, like Luc. Will he be put on a plane back to Kinshasa too? I ask.

'Don't worry Chipo,' David says, 'Jean-Paul has already been here ten years and has asylum-seeker status.'

'It is you and I who should worry,' George tells me. 'Our six months will be up in two weeks' time.'

When George and I went back to Home Affairs, George was even more nervous than the first time. Me too. But everything went smoothly. We didn't get any nasty surprises, and the lady behind the counter told me my decision was 'still pending'.

Until Home Affairs makes its final decision, Peter says we are on borrowed time. But the good news is that some people can wait as long as four years to hear the outcome of their application. There is a backlog at Home Affairs, says Peter, and not enough motivated staff to sort out the piles of paper. So we might be OK. In four years we could achieve a lot.

George doesn't agree. He says that even though we received another six-month permit, it doesn't mean much because the World Cup is coming. And that might be the end of us. I know he is combing his brain trying to figure out a clever plan to earn lots of rand fast. But so far he is still stuck sweeping dead cockroaches out of Mr Ross's kitchen and washing street children's shit off the pavements.

'We could try to sell something?' Peter suggests. 'Some foreigners have started to do a side trade in World Cup memorabilia.'

This is true. I see them leaving President's Heights early in the mornings with miniature South African flags to sell to the motorists travelling to work.

George shakes his head. 'Ha, waste of time. Selling flags is not going to save anyone's backside. And you know what is most pathetic of all?' George raises his voice so that Jeremiah, who is standing near the window, can hear. 'Those foreign Africans who have started wearing Bafana Bafana jerseys like they are natives.'

Jeremiah flinches like someone has just spilt boiling tea on his hand. He is wearing the green and yellow national team shirt with the collar turned up.

'They think that if they wear South Africa's team jersey, that makes them real South Africans. They think it will keep them safe. Ha. No one cares what soccer shirt you wear. They only care what your "pass book" says.'

That's what George has started to call our Home Affairs papers. Pass book. He says that when the whites still ruled South Africa, all the blacks had to carry a pass book. The pass book said who could go where and when.

'Exaggeration,' says David. 'Our documents are no apartheid pass book.'

But George goes on and on. It is rare for him to show that he too was no fool at school before lack of money forced us to stop attending.

∼

'We are going to Fabric City.' Jean-Paul is pulling on his coat when I come in.

Fabric City? In Woodstock? I want to talk to Jean-Paul about everything. About pass books. About Luc. About whether to worry now that the rumour has spread. But I know that he never goes anywhere if he can help it. So this must be important. I go fetch my jacket and together we walk down to the bottom of Long Street to catch a minibus taxi.

When we reach the corner of Sir Lowry Road, the taxi door slides open and Jean-Paul and I get out.

'What *is* that noise they are always playing?' Jean-Paul grimaces as the taxi speeds off, the windows rattling with local hip-hop. 'Shout shout. I don't know.' He shakes his head like he never heard such music back in the Congo.

Jean-Paul longs for a quiet life, I think, as I watch him walking slowly up the street towards Fabric City, leaning on his cane. He must be a man more used to the rural life – its soft sounds and way of doing things. Everything about the city seems to bother him. The crowds, the dirt, the noise. What was it like, the place where he grew up? I wish he would tell me.

Fabric City is a large shop that sells nothing but cloth. Some bolts are for upholstery, some for curtains, but the majority are for clothes. It is the place where Jean-Paul usually sends his customers. It is very unusual for him to go himself, so I am curious. When we step through the door, we are immediately greeted by the owner.

'Mr Jean-Paul! A welcome surprise. How are you?'

'Fine, fine, Ashraf. And you? Business good?'

'Very good, thank you, my friend, Allah be praised. Jamal, bring a chair.'

A young boy, no more than twelve or thirteen, hurries over with a chair and Jean-Paul gratefully slumps into it.

'What can we help you with today, Jean-Paul?'

'We've come for the young lady.'

For me?

'For me, Jean-Paul?' I turn to look at him.

'Today is your birthday, is it not, Chipo? Eighteen is an important age…'

I nod. Blush. He is the only one who has remembered. I knew he would not forget.

'You are growing up. And a young lady requires a winter wardrobe. But first you must choose the fabric.' Jean-Paul turns to Ashraf. 'Show us your best winter fabrics.'

Ashraf takes us to the far end of the shop. On wide tables there are large rolls of fabric all piled one on top of the other.

'Here on the left. Natural fabrics. More expensive, but in the end,' Ashraf lowers his voice, 'better value.'

'Excellent. Which colours, Chipo?'

I look. Pinks, blues, yellows, greens. Some are sari fabrics that the Indians like. Gold with black trim. Black with gold butterflies. Others have African patterns. I look at Jean-Paul. He is too kind to hurry me, but I am sure he is growing impatient to get back to his room. I turn back to the bolts of fabric, as colourful as fruit and vegetables at market. Which one should I choose? I feel overwhelmed by so much choice. It isn't often in my life that I am asked, 'What would you like, Chipo?' 'Which would you prefer?'

'I don't know which to choose.'

Jean-Paul waves his hand. 'Something bright. No hiding in the shadows, my child.'

I point to a blue and a red. The blue one has tiny yellow dots on it, the red one small white flowers.

'Excellent choice. Ashraf, five metres of each.'

Ashraf clicks his fingers for one of his young assistants. He is a Muslim like Ashraf. Short and thin, with thick black hair and high cheekbones.

He picks up each bolt of cloth in turn and, with an expert gesture, rolls it out onto an empty table. Using a long wooden ruler and a pair of metal scissors, the sort that Jean-Paul uses, he begins to cut. Not once does he look at Jean-Paul or myself. But when he has finished he presents the fabric, neatly folded, to his boss. Then he returns to his sewing machine, where, I can see, he is making a suit.

Jean-Paul pays and I watch the young man as he hurries through his work, the machine's needle humming between his hands. Hanging behind him on the wall is an example of his craftsmanship. A grey suit and a yellow dress. Their suits are not half as good as what Jean-Paul produces, I think to myself with pride as we take our plastic bags of fabric and walk back to the corner to wait for a taxi.

'A cold day,' complains Jean-Paul as we walk. 'In my country, one never gets chilled to the bone...'

'What do you miss most about home?' I ask.

'Our garden.'

'What was it like?'

'Always colourful. My wife loved to grow flowers. She made sure something was always in bloom.'

It is the first time Jean-Paul has spoken about her. The woman in the photograph. I cannot resist.

'What was her name, Jean-Paul?'

'She was called Marie.'

Was. So she *is* dead. I want to tell him that I know what it is like. But just then the taxi comes and I know Jean-Paul won't want to talk in a crowded taxi.

Back at President's Heights, in Jean-Paul's room, I think of Mama. She liked to garden too.

'What are those seeds, Amai?'

'Pumpkin, *mwanangu*. I have been saving them for when the weather is good. Pass me the spade.'

'How deep do seeds need to be planted?'

'Different seeds require different depths. Some are strong. They can be buried deep. Others need to be near the surface where they can feel the warmth.'

'And pumpkin seeds?'

'Pumpkin seeds are hardy. They can go as deep as your little finger. Come and look. You must put them this way up.'

I watch Mama plop the seeds into the soil with spaces in between. Then she covers them with a layer of soil, pats the soil down and waters them. I know that in a few weeks little green shoots will come, fine as blades of grass. Later the blades will grow thick like tendrils. Leaves will appear and finally the pumpkins themselves, orange as sunsets. When you knock on them they sound hollow when they are ready to be harvested. Then we will cut them free one at a time, carry them inside and store them on top of the kitchen cupboard.

I liked to garden as a girl, though I had to be careful of the sun.

'Have you put on your sun lotion?'

'Yes, Mama.'

'Let me see. OK. Pull your hat lower.'

Mama taught me that certain plants prefer to be harvested at different times of the day. Chomolia, for example. That likes to be picked early, when the day is still cool. If not, it wilts. Tomatoes too. Pumpkins can be harvested at any time. We made pumpkin soup or roasted it. I liked to eat it with a lump of butter and sprinkled with sugar. When I was young, Mama told me I had a sweet tooth.

Looking down from the window in Jean-Paul's room, after we have returned home from Fabric City, I imagine Long Street transformed into a strip of fertile agricultural land, with soil dark as wet coffee grounds. George and I are not country people. We lived in a location. Still, I cannot help but imagine. I squint until I can see the concrete replaced with soil that has been dug up and planted. The people walking below with handbags and cellphones, I imagine them carrying spades and hoes. The cars become tractors. The traffic lights, trees. I imagine myself standing at the top of Long Street and, looking down, seeing a road of maize. Tall green shoots with white mealie heads for as far as the eye can see. I imagine this farm running all the way down to the sea. It would be calm. The pace, slow.

Sea rhymes with Marie. I turn to look at the photograph. Today, white roses, their petals opened wide in the little vase. I can hear Jean-Paul's voice, saying, 'Marie, marry me.'

Was he romantic? Did he surprise her? Were they young? What did Jean-Paul look like when he was a young man? Was his foot already lame? Was Marie the sort of woman who fell in love with a man even if he possessed an infirmity?

I imagine the seated woman in the photograph smiling down at Jean-Paul on one knee on the grass. They are outside. He has taken her for a walk. Away from the prying eyes of their parents. A walk to look at the flowers. Then, when she stops to admire one of her favourites, Jean-Paul takes her hand. That high forehead and thin angular face are surprised at first. Of course, she was expecting him to propose at some point. They have been seeing each other for more than a year, after all, and her family is starting to ask questions. But she has been caught off guard. She is wearing a fuchsia-coloured blouse and a yellow skirt similar in cut to the white blouse and green skirt she is wearing in the photograph. Nothing covers her head. Her hair is short, black and curly, done in the natural style, a style that she will never change because he tells her he likes her hair that way. She is laughing. Her eyes are scrunched up with happiness.

'Well? Are you going to keep me waiting? Yes or no?'

She says yes. And from that yes comes a wedding and later the child in the photograph, too. A girl. In the photo she is not much older than eleven. She looks like Jean-Paul. Her face is round. Her eyes large. She is frowning. Her mouth pouts. She has Jean-Paul's temper.

In the background of the photo one can see a blur of emerald green. Trees? Or Marie's garden?

Sometimes when I visit him now, after all that has happened, I see that Jean-Paul is still living in a city, yes, but he has a room right at the very top of the tallest apartment building he could find. When he looks out of his bedroom window, all he can see is blue sky and clouds and, when it grows dark, the strange starless sky of city nights. He has to look down to see the cars and the bustle of urban life. The pedestrians and minibus taxis. They are like distant irritations. He has created a garden on the flat roof of that building, too, among the television aerials, crooked like scarecrows. A garden sown in pots and all sorts of discarded containers. Some are metal, some wood. There are even old tyres. And in them Jean-Paul grows flowers and vegetables: tomatoes, spinach, onions and all manner of greenery, thick like sea foam. A rural garden up in the urban sky. That is what my old friend has made for himself in his new home. That is where he escapes and talks to ghosts. Sometimes, on clear days, he stands on that roof and feels the warmth carried by the concrete and the breeze. He imagines that in the distance he can see his home country and, within its borders, his village. He stands and looks. Then turns away. No, he cannot go back. Even if they have forgotten his face, he has not forgotten theirs.

But such gardens were still far away that afternoon when Jean-Paul and I made our way to Fabric City and he told me for the first time of his wife who liked nothing better than fresh flowers cut from her own garden.

'OK, everyone, have a good evening. I'm going out.'

David looks handsome. He is freshly showered and is wearing a red V-neck jersey and pressed black trousers.

'Who are you going with?'

Peter is standing in front of David, blocking his access to the front door. He came home early today in a strange mood and has been drinking for the past three hours. In his hand there is a litre bottle of Castle Lager. It is almost empty.

David looks at his brother, confused and a little offended.

'What do you mean, who am I going with? I am not five years old, you know, and you are not our parents.'

David smiles, but Peter doesn't smile. His expression is tight and serious.

'Are you going with Jeremiah?'

David shakes his head and looks exasperated. 'Yes, I am going with Jeremiah.'

'And where are you going?'

'Oh, fuck off, Peter. This is ridiculous.' David tries to push past, but Peter stands firm.

George and I are watching this from across the room from our seats by the kitchen table. We both look at each other. We have never seen the brothers behave in this manner before. George shrugs his shoulders.

David stands up straighter and grits his teeth. He is clearly extremely irritated but is trying not to show it. Peter, a little drunk, sways in the doorway.

'We are going to a bar, brother,' David replies, his voice a dangerous hiss.

The two brothers are staring straight into each other's eyes. Identical twins, I think to myself, but so different. Peter's eyelid is hanging even lower than usual because of the drink. He has taken off his work shirt and is standing barefoot, in just his vest and jeans. There is some sort of brown stain on his vest. David would never do that. Stand around in dirty clothes. I can't look at Peter. He shouldn't be speaking to David like this.

George shakes his head and lights a cigarette. I watch the tip of it glow red. George tosses the match onto his empty plate and leans back. His cellphone beeps and he picks it up.

'Tell me, what sort of bars do you and your friend Jeremiah go to, hey? Not the bars on Long Street. So what bars?'

But this is one question too many for David. He pushes past his brother and slams the door behind him.

George opens his mouth to speak, but Peter holds up his hand to indicate no. No questions. Peter switches on the television and sits down on a crate. He turns up the volume so that talking is impossible.

I bite my lip. I do not want David to go out with Jeremiah tonight either. I want him to stay with me. But still, I do not understand Peter's rude behaviour.

George is sucking on his cigarette and composing an SMS.

'George?' I say softly.

He gives me a look as if to say *We are all on edge* and goes back to his SMS.

Later, when David gets back I ask him in private: 'Where do you and Jeremiah go, when you go out together?'

But David does not like my question. He is vague: 'Where? Oh, here and there. Sometimes to, you know, a film.'

I am a slave to my curiosity. I need to know, even though I can see it is annoying David.

'Come now, Chipo, no more questions. I need to sleep, OK?'

And then David stops coming home some nights.

I wake in the night. A thought is troubling me. The girl in Jean-Paul's photo. The daughter. What happened to her?

Twelve

Another week. Another step closer to the World Cup. I have overheard whispering. People stand in groups in Mountain Dew and talk in low, nervous voices. In the queues at the taxi rank, they speak in their own languages – languages they know the locals cannot understand.

'What should we do? Should we stay or go?'

As I pass the cafés and bars, young men, seated around tables on the pavement, debate in low, serious voices over their beer or Coca-Cola.

In my mind, I imagine what they are saying. Is it better to go now? Before any troubles? Should they just throw away everything? The new lives they have created?

We in the flat try to keep busy.

One night, David and Jeremiah stay in to play chess. Jeremiah is laughing. David has made a foolish error.

'Five moves, my friend. Five moves and checkmate! A world record!'

He is laughing so hard his eyes are watering. It looks like he is crying.

Choirboy hangs his arm around his friend and, still laughing, pulls him close. He looks like he is embracing David, like he is pulling David to his heart.

～

Jeremiah rhymes with 'love thy neighbour'. The Bible commands, 'Love thy neighbour as thyself'. Mama read that passage to us, and other passages too. Not often, but when she did we were expected to pay attention. I remember her sitting with her Bible on her lap, quietly reading to herself one afternoon. She was already sick but we didn't know it yet. But I see it now, looking back. I see her skirt held up with a belt that every few months she was forced to tighten by another notch. Old Trafford was gone and she made a meagre living selling rock buns at the bus terminus. She was sitting on the large plastic bucket with a lid that she sold her buns from. It was a good day – she had sold almost all of them. The rest would be our dinner.

She is sitting in the half-light, reading by the window. The breeze causes the onion-skin pages to rustle. She has not taken off her woollen hat or jacket. She is cold all the time. She is tired. Outside, the evening noise has begun. Music is filtering through open doorways – gospel and rumba imported from the Congo, as people try to dance and drink away their sorrows. But Mama is reading. And as she reads, she weeps.

These are difficult weeks. The sky seems permanently overcast. So do our moods. Sometimes Jean-Paul will fall into one of his depressions. These last longer than before. Three, even four days. I worry he will disappear for good, like water sucked down the plughole.

I have no one to talk to when Jean-Paul's door is closed. David is always with Choirboy when he is not working, and Peter and George only have time for their women and the television.

I don't know how my brother coped before this television came into his life. Sometimes I think he needs it to pump oxygen into his lungs.

'We work hard. We need our rest,' he says defensively.

Then he tells me to fetch him a beer from the fridge, quick-quick. If Jean-Paul isn't working, he makes a point of adding, 'since you've got nothing to do'. I don't know how he thinks his dinner gets made and his shirts washed.

'Maybe Mr Congo needs a head doctor,' George said the last time Jean-Paul was under the weather. But I told him straight that there is nothing wrong with Jean-Paul and that George shouldn't talk that way about his elders. Then I added that Mama would be vexed if she heard him being so disrespectful. That always tends to shut George up. I don't think he likes the idea of Mama's spirit looking down on him, disappointed by his lax manners. Also, Jean-Paul always pays me, no matter what. He is a man of his word, and that deserves respect.

After I have finished my chores, and if Jean-Paul is locked in his room, I try to keep myself busy by watching what is happening on Long Street. Once or twice I have taken myself back to the art museum. When I go, I talk to David in my head or I think of clever things to say about those paintings and lumps of metal so that, next time we go, he will know that I have more than samp for brains. George doesn't mind where I go these days, so long as I don't spend money. He says we've got to save in case the manure falls from the sky in July after all.

'We need to prepare for the worst.'

The worst sounds like thirst. Every day these past six months, my thirst for David has grown worse and worse. David says there are horses that live in Namibia, the country north of South Africa, who have learnt to live in the desert with nothing but stones to eat. But I am not such an animal. I need more.

'Let's go to the science museum. Please, David.'

And my heart lights up as though a thousand watts of electricity run through it when he agrees. That is where we are walking to now. To the museum. I want him to touch me. He is standing right beside me, so all I would need to do would be to lean a little to the left. But I am afraid that then he will know all that I have brewing inside. What I have stirring feels more potent than any batch of Mama's Seven Days beer. I turn to look at the cars. When I watch their wheels as they pass, how fast they spin, I become dizzy, then frightened. David is still talking. Recently he has said that he would like to become a teacher.

'Secondary school.'

School sounds like fool. Sin sounds like spin. Christians believe that sin sends you spinning down to hell. That is what they teach in Sunday school. If you just take his hand, Chipo...

The robot's red man turns green. We cross. The sign of the cross is supposed to protect you from evil spirits. Mama did believe that. It can bring luck too. Before Manchester United played, Mama would make the sign of the cross. It gives you quick access to God.

When I was six and George nine, George believed he could run super-fast. For two whole months, he made me time him as he ran the length of our street and back again.

'How... fast?'

'Seventy-two.'

'What? That's slower than last time. Learn how to count properly.'

He had seen a programme on television about a bionic man. Then, when he came third on sports day, he stopped believing.

Inside the museum there are many wonders, like the rare bones of dinosaurs and dead animals stuffed so that they look alive but frozen in time. But all I can think of is David. He is talking about this and that. He points to the skeleton of a giant fish. It hangs across the entire ceiling, big as a shack.

'That's a whale. Largest mammals on earth. People called them Leviathans. They travel past Cape Town on their way to Antarctica.'

There is a small chamber. When you sit inside it you can hear whales singing to one another. Their songs sound full of longing.

'Did you ever want to study at university, Chipo?'

'I wanted to be a nurse, or a social worker.'

'You could go back to school, you know. You would make a fine social worker.'

I remember Jean-Paul's client. The one from Ghana who wants to be a nurse.

'May I tell you a secret?'

A secret? My heart stirs.

'Of course, David. You know I can be trusted.'

'I know, Chipo. In you, I feel I have found another sister.'

'A sister…?'

'Jeremiah and I are planning on going back to university. To the University of the Western Cape. UWC. We met some students. They came to the restaurant and told us about applying. Anyway, this time I will apply to do literature and education. Like I always wanted.'

'That's wonderful, David.'

Sister? Like a sister? Is that what he said?

Sister. Spinster. On the way home, David stops in front of a shop window. There is a T-shirt for sale. Its slogan reads: 'A Woman Needs a Man Like a Fish Needs a Bicycle'. On it there is a drawing of a fish pedalling a bicycle.

'I can understand why some women feel that way,' David says, standing in front of the window. 'Most men are not worth the trouble.'

'If I were a fish I would want you for my bicycle.'

David looks at me, surprised, and laughs.

'You are a true eccentric, Chipo! Come, I had better get you home before George worries.'

Later in the afternoon David comes home with a carrier bag full of second-hand books from Clarke's bookshop. Poetry and a collection of plays. Writers I have never heard of. David arranges them very carefully in a pile.

'I am going to start with Athol Fugard's *The Island*. No man is an island. That is a famous expression.'

'David. I would like to, the thing is, what I was trying to say earlier, outside the shop—'

'I have met this girl at the restaurant, Chipo. A student on the course. She told me what they are reading. I thought I would start. Jeremiah says it's good to be prepared, and I think he's right.'

My blood runs cold. *A woman*?

'Is she… What is her name?'

'Patience.'

Patience is a virtue.

'Is she, is she pretty?'

'What? Yes, I suppose.'

David's cellphone rings.

'Hello? Hi, yes yes. See you tonight. Wouldn't miss it. One second… Chipo?'

I have locked myself in the bathroom. From inside I hear David say, 'Oh, she's gone. I wanted to ask her about my black trousers…'

Mismatch.
Misread.
Misrepresent.
Misaim.
Misfire.
Misspent.
Mistake.

Mistake sounds like break. Sometimes we break something by mistake.

Thirteen

The student. She is all I can think about. Patience rhymes with? Sounds like? Patience is a virtue. What does she look like? Talk like, laugh like, smell like? She talks into his ear. Smiles. He smiles back. Thinks about burying his nose in her neck. That evening I burn the rice and do not stir in the peanut butter. When I wash the dishes, one slips onto the floor and cracks. I stop and leave the pots and remaining dishes in a dripping heap. He didn't mean to hurt you, Chipo. That is what I try to tell myself as I pick up the broken pieces and drop them into the bin.

I go and stand by the window. Everyone is out, as usual. They ate and left, leaving Tortoise to do their cleaning. George is at the restaurant, where he is working night shifts this week. Peter is no doubt in a bar. And David? Where is *he*?

Patience is a woman of lax virtue. What kind of woman throws herself at waiters in restaurants? The kind who exposes an immodest cleavage.

From the window I can see it. The night they met. Is she white? A *murungu* who likes her chocolate dark? No, David would never go for that. She is an African, for sure. A local girl with an appetite for exotic *amakwerekwere* flavours? Or could she even be from Zimbabwe? A homegirl like me? No, not like you, Chipo. Nothing like you. I see them now. She has asked him to meet her at a bar. Somewhere in this city. Maybe even on Long Street. Her. David talking to her. She will be sitting at the bar, drinking like a prostitute. Skirt very short. He will admire her jacket. Her legs. Her skin. I see it. I know it. David mouthing the words into her neck, 'Hmmm, *mambokadzi*, you smell so good. Let's see each other again tomorrow.'

By the time David finally comes in, tiptoeing like a thief, I feel as though a hand has squeezed all the blood from my heart. I can no longer think in sentences. Only words. She. Him. Them.

The next morning, I cannot speak. Do not dare to feel. My heart feels soaked in vinegar. I dress and wash automatically. Make breakfast. I do not greet David when he wakes. As soon as I can, I leave the flat to deliver Jean-Paul's clothes.

After the last delivery, I decide not to go back. I need to walk. I think about George squeezing mango juice for the General's wife on that last afternoon, when the General's jealousy came trembling across the tiles to the servants' quarters. He threw her out. Threw her out for humiliating him and forcing him to expose his jealousy. Jealousy sounds like melody. There is no melody in my heart. Only a violent, noisy hopelessness. No one will ever marry you, *soooope*.

A memory. There is shouting outside. I am twelve. Two boys, primary-school age, are fighting in the dirt, pulling at each other's school shirts. They both fall into a heap, and the smallest is punching the other boy's chest as their soccer ball rolls away from them and their school bags spill their exercise books.

'Ha, you are last, so you must marry Chipo!'

'I will *not* marry Chipo.'

'Yes, you will. That was the bet. And you are last!'

The small boy looks at the other, looks at me and kicks dirt into his friend's face.

'I WILL NOT MARRY CHIPO!'

I walk down the pavement, my eyes on the ground. I don't even care about the crowds of shoppers and office workers pushing past me. Some stare. Some always stare.

It feels like the very air is a burden. Weight sounds like hate. Like fate. Miserable sounds like terrible. Only it is worse. Much, much worse. Worse always comes first.

I reach the corner of Adderley and Darling. I stop and wait for the man to jump from red to green. Just then a hand offers me a piece of paper. I look up. The hand belongs to a young woman. A local. She's not even looking at who she is handing her pieces of paper to. Her eyes are closed. She is listening to the music playing on her cellphone, singing aloud to herself. No doubt dreaming of one day being a famous music star. Ha ha. Sorry for her.

Does she look like David's woman? NO, I must not call her that. There is still a chance. Ha. NO CHANCE, *SOPE*. Patience does not look like this girl. Fat, with pimples. Still, I feel a mixture of hatred and envy towards paper-slip girl. Two conflicting emotions, like cooking oil mixed with water. But I take the piece of paper she blindly offers. Bringing it close to my nose, I read:

DOCTOR ONGANI

CONSULTATION FEE R50.00

STOP SUFFERING

1) Get *amagundwane* for riches
2) Recover stolen property (2 hrs)
3) Court cases/divorce cases
4) Do you need protection at home/work?
5) Do you need to be promoted at work?
6) Do you need clients?
7) Do you need to increase your payslip?
8) Do you need to reduce your vagina/increase your penis?

I blush but continue.

9) Get lost lover back (1 day) guaranteed
10) Get right partner. Win loved one (7 days) guaranteed

THE MIRACLE MEDICINES THAT CANNOT FAIL

I think: yes, I *am* suffering. I think: this Doctor Ongani offers miracles. I need a miracle. I think: win loved one. Seven days. I think of David. I think about that woman growing on him like a weed that will soon swallow him and leave nothing for me. There is a telephone number on the piece of paper. I take out my cellphone and dial it.

'Hello?'

'Hello, Doctor Ongani?'

'Yes, speak up, I cannot hear you.' In the background, a sound like someone sanding wood.

'I have your advertisement… you say you can help with matters of the heart.'

'Ah yes. Apologies. Renovations going on over here. What sort of matters?'

'I... want someone to fall in love with me.'

'I require something that belongs to him. Something from his body. A piece of hair or a fingernail will do. The fee will be a hundred and fifty ZARs.'

'But your advertisement says fifty ZARs.'

'That was a special price. A sale price. The sale ended yesterday. Would you like a consultation or not?'

I think about this. This might be my only chance to get David before the other woman devours him. Devoured sounds like tired. I am tired. Tired of hoping. Tired of trying. But I am not ready to give up. I will beg Jean-Paul for the money. Tell him I am sick.

'I want a consultation.'

'Twenty St George's Mall. Tenth floor. Room 1080. Tomorrow at ten.'

When the others are out that evening, I go through David's things. One by one I examine his shirts, his jerseys, his jackets. How is it that there is not a single hair? Then I open the tin that contains his comb, his razor, his deodorant. Thank God. A single tiny hair is caught in the teeth of the comb. Very carefully, I pick it off.

The next morning I make an excuse to Jean-Paul. Terrible stomach cramps. I grip my stomach.

'I need medicine. But the pharmacy says it costs one hundred and fifty.'

Jean-Paul looks concerned. 'Are they certain it is not your appendix? You must be careful of your appendix, you know. Are you nauseous?'

I shake my head. 'No, just cramps,' I moan. 'I am sure it is not my appendix.'

Jean-Paul goes to the tin in his cupboard where he keeps his money. I know that it is a sign that he trusts me.

'Here, go immediately.'

Relieved that my story worked, but still clutching my stomach, I hurry out.

I find Doctor Ongani's building without trouble. It is tall and grey. A shabbier building than those around it. I ride the rattling lift to the tenth floor and ring the doorbell. A minute or two pass before I hear the chain being slid on the other side. The door opens a crack.

'Yes?' I recognise the voice, although I cannot yet see him.

'Doctor Ongani?'

'Yes.'

'We spoke on the phone. I have an appointment.'

The door opens. My first impressions of the Doctor are that he is shorter than I expected. He has a beard and small blue eyes, like our President back home. Some say that those black Africans with the rare gift of blue eyes are destined for great things. He directs me inside.

'Come in.'

Doctor Ongani's office is small and pretty bare except for a desk with two chairs, one of which has the seat padding bursting out. Still, the Doctor himself looks respectable, I tell myself. He is wearing a black suit. In the corner, a purple curtain conceals a back room. On the wall of his office there is a leopard skin, pinned up like a map.

'Please, sit. So how can I be of assistance, Miss...?'

'Chipo.'

The Doctor smiles. Two of his top teeth are gold. 'Miss Chipo. You mentioned something about love?'

I sit while the Doctor listens to my problem.

'Have you brought what I asked?'

I open the envelope in which I have carefully kept the precious hair. I pass it to the Doctor. I watch as he examines it.

'Good. Now I must consult the ancestors.'

He closes his eyes and begins to murmur. It reminds me of the mutterings within the New Jerusalem Church back home. Every Sunday you could hear the uproar as members of the congregation, possessed by the Holy Spirit, babbled in tongues not their own. After a few moments, the Doctor stops.

'The ancestors are sympathetic. I can help.'

Fourteen

But nothing happens. Day one. Day two. Three, four, five, six, seven, eight! I waited for David to look at me differently. Seven days guaranteed? Ha!

'Return my hundred and fifty,' I told the Doctor over the phone. I unleashed all my anguish about David onto him and accused him of trying to cheat me.

Doctor Ongani remained calm. He sounded surprised. 'You need to follow David. This other girl – she must have put a spell on him.'

'A spell?'

'Yes. Do you think you are the only one who uses witch doctors?'

A spell! Suddenly it all made sense. David was not himself. He was *bewitched*. Bewitched sounds like switched. Back home, some people believed that if a person suddenly changed his behaviour, acted out of character, or if particularly bad luck befell the family, something supernatural was afoot. It might be a jealous aunt or uncle. It might even be the mischief of a ghost.

'Don't be ridiculous,' were Mama's words when I told her what Humility at school was saying. That someone had put a curse on her cousin and that was why she failed her O-levels.

'Humility's cousin failed her O-levels because that cousin of hers is as dumb as dirt. No one put a curse on anyone.'

'But Humility says—'

'I do not care what Humility says. She is telling stories.'

'But—'

'Chipo. No more. Help me with these boiled eggs.'

'Yes, Amai.'

Mama never let me tell her the full story. Of how it was said that Humility's cousin fell down in church and started foaming at the mouth. How she spoke such filthy words that it was clear that some or other demon had taken possession of her. And if it could happen to Humility's cousin, then why not David?

I know that Mama did believe in ghosts. Once she told us about a friend whose family was haunted by troubles because they had not performed the *kurova guva* ritual. Even the Christians do it. After Mama died, Aunt Ruth made sure Mama got it. If you don't, the spirit can't go and rest with the ancestors and it becomes very restless, even angry.

Restless, homeless ghosts are not the same as bewitchment, but Doctor Ongani's story about David... I need to believe it. So I do as Doctor Ongani ordered. I follow David that very night. I do it for love.

'I must deliver a suit to a security guard. He needs it tonight. I must go out.' But George is hardly listening. WWE title contest. Mr Power versus the Maniac.

I hide inside the doorway of the superette and wait for David to stop a minibus taxi and get in.

'Quick,' I ask a lady after he has gone. 'Where is that taxi going?'

'Green Point, Sea Point. That direction.'

'I need to follow it.'

The lady looks me up and down like I have trouble in my brain, but she says, 'That one over there is going to the same place.'

'Thank you, *sisi*.'

I make it onto the other taxi just in time. Thankfully the driver speeds. And thanks to the traffic lights turning green in our favour, I find myself only a few cars behind David.

He jumps out and goes into a small bar. So this is where he meets her. His Patience.

'Please,' I beg the large coloured man at the door, 'my brother has just gone inside and his wife is giving birth.'

He frowned. 'We don't want that sort of trouble here.'

'Please. I will make no trouble. I promise.'

'Yessus. OK, tell me your brother's name and what he looks like and I will fetch him…'

I shake my head.

'Then I cannot help you. I am sorry. Please step back and let the others through.'

I do as I am told. What now? Can I find a way to sneak in? I watch the queue move. There are only men in the line. Most are white. A few coloured. Even fewer who are black. What sort of bar is this? I look up and read the sign. Crew. A rainbow flag flutters beside it. I have heard South Africa described as the 'rainbow nation'. Was this a bar only for South Africans? And if so, how has David gained entry?

'Excuse me,' I ask a thin white man at the back of the queue. He has blond hair and a kind, paternal face and I do not think he will mind me asking. 'What sort of bar is this? Is it only for South Africans?'

The man frowns. 'Are you serious?'

I nod.

'It's a gay bar, my darling.'

'Gay?'

'Jesus, where are you from? A bar for homos… You know, *moffies*? We children of the homosexual persuasion…'

'But David isn't a homosexual.'

'David? African? Tall? Nice eyes? From Zimbabwe?'

I nod again.

'Oh, my darling, your David is a full-blown sister. He was shy at first, kept to himself. But now he comes here with his friend. Another African. Can't remember his name… Do you want me to tell him you are looking for him?'

I stand frozen. David and this man know each other? David frequenting a bar for homosexuals? The man looks at me.

I shake my head. 'No, no, it's OK.'

I leave the man. My head is spinning. David… an *ngochani*? No. I shake my head. I can't believe it.

Moffie
Buttock Beak
Homo
Homosexual
Pédé
Gay
Festering Finger
Ngochani

'Twenty-eight rand for two avocados! Can you believe it?' Jeremiah shakes his head. 'And to think I ate them for free by the dozen when I was a boy visiting my cousins in the country.'

George yawns. He is watching *Isidingo*. He leans forward and turns up the volume. But David nods.

'Inflation.'

He and Jeremiah are playing chess again. David has yet to win a game, but Jeremiah has teased that today might be David's lucky day.

'Well,' Jeremiah continues, as he watches David's hand hover over one piece, then another, 'we are all Zimbabweans here. High food prices should come as no surprise. But I never expected it to be so expensive in South Africa.'

'They say the Chinese have a hand in it.' David makes his move and Jeremiah nods his approval. David looks so pleased. It's just a crumb, David, I think bitterly to myself. David's finger drums the plastic table. Jeremiah's hand is just by it. Close enough to touch it. Does he want to touch it? Stroke his friend's hand? Festering fingers. Isn't that what the government called their sort back in '98? Festering fingers. Ngochanes. Buttock Beaks. What would you two do if everyone knew you were *that sort*? And you, Choirboy? If the others knew? Peter and George would beat you until you couldn't walk. No more chess for you two. No more anything at all, I think.

David and Jeremiah continue to chatter. I hear them laugh. Once or twice I think I catch them looking at each other, secretly, smiling the way a man and wife should. From the place where I am folding the washing I can watch David, unobserved. I see it now. The way he looks at Jeremiah. It is hunger.

When I was a child, a vagrant once came to the door asking for food. He was very thin and one of his legs was missing, so that he hobbled on a crutch. Mama was inside when he knocked and she gave him three avocados and half a loaf of bread.

'Poor soul,' Mama said when the bundle of rags had hobbled off. 'Who knows when last he ate a proper meal?'

I had hidden when the man came, but now I spied on him from the window. As soon as he was a respectable distance from our house he leaned against an electricity pole and, with incredible care, began to peel an avocado. First he bit into the top and, making sure that he had sucked all the sweet, creamy flesh from that piece, dropped it. Then, slowly, with caressing and gentle hands, he began to peel the rest. Before he discarded a piece of skin he made sure to suck the last bit of flesh from it. He even licked the stone.

I felt guilty watching. But having not yet known hunger myself at that age, I could not stop. With each bite he took, he closed his eyes. Relish. His bites were big but he chewed slowly. Eyes closed. Almost a smile. Was he remembering happy times when avocados were plentiful? Or the person who, all those years before, gave them to him? Perhaps his own mother?

When I look at David now, whenever he is with Jeremiah, I see that same expression. Every word, every moment Jeremiah offers up to him, David takes it, peels it slowly and devours it as though each word, each gesture, were meeting a hunger so deep, so private, that only Jeremiah has the medicine to satisfy it. And Jeremiah? His eyes sparkle when he looks at David. Their hands on the table. So close they are almost touching. Fingers. Festering fingers.

I go to the toilet. I look at my face in the mirror. My *sope* face. Flushed. The face of a fool. To think. David and you. Meanwhile, all along... Fool. You have made a fool of yourself! A thorn is caught in my throat. You will not cry. That is what I tell myself, but my eyes are filling with water. I can feel the saliva gathering in my mouth and my throat growing tight. In spite of my promise to myself, tears begin to roll down my cheeks.

Fifteen

David is upset. He will not say why. But I know why. His Choirboy is gone. He will not play chess with David. Will not take his calls, his SMSes. Has quit his job at the restaurant and disappeared. Leaving no forwarding address and no means to get in touch.

All day long David has lain on his mattress and refused to speak with anyone. This past hour, Peter has been trying to get David out of bed but the most he has managed, after some effort, is to get his brother to sit up. Peter wants to talk. About soccer. About a man who came into the bead shop wearing a suit and an expensive watch.

'He bought a kilo of *everything*. Can you imagine? Even the Swarovski crystal beads, and those cost, what-what, hundreds *each*. I wanted to say to him, "Don't waste your money on this rubbish, rich man. Give it to me instead…"'

'What is *wrong* with you?' Peter is getting impatient with his brother now. 'Are you listening to me?'

'Woman trouble?' burps George.

I cannot help but laugh. The three turn to look at me. I want to say, 'I know. I know what is haunting him.' But it is a secret. And I am responsible for it.

I had gone back to see Doctor Ongani. Sat in his small dark

office. Outside, some workers were putting up scaffolding, and clanged and banged while the Doctor and I talked.

'Do you possess a cure for a man who loves another man but who you want to love you?'

'There is a cure for everything. But first you must get rid of the other man. This Jeremiah. Is he a gay too?'

I nodded. 'He is very religious, but I think so.'

'Ah,' said Doctor Ongani with a smile, as he leaned forward, elbows on the table, 'that's easy, then.'

He went to the little room where he kept his bottles and buckets of herbs and animal parts, their secrets concealed by the purple curtain.

'The *muti*. Very powerful. Eighty rand.'

I opened my purse. I did not have enough. I already owed the Doctor two hundred rand.

'Do not worry. We will find a way for you to pay me.'

I should have seen it then, what he had in store for me. But I was too desperate. Too blinded by jealousy. I took the small parcel wrapped in newspaper.

'Oh, Chipo, include a letter.'

That was what Doctor Ongani told me. 'A letter from someone anonymous to the other man. A letter, say, from a member of his church warning him that you have discovered all about him and David. Tell him that if he doesn't end it immediately, you will let the whole community know what sort of homosexual filth he has got up to. Deliver it, but don't let the other man know it is you who has delivered it. Then place the *muti* under your David's mattress. Once the man is gone, come back and I will help you win your David.'

In the stairwell I had sniffed it. It smelt like the grey dust you find under a cupboard.

David still refuses to speak.

'You are so secretive about your girls. If I didn't know you better, I would say that you only like to go with the married ones. Beat him! Call yourself Iron Man? Get him!' George punches the air, then sits down, captivated by the wrestling. The crowd in the television set roars.

David doesn't respond. Peter speaks for him: 'That's right. Only the married ones. Isn't that so, brother?'

David looks at Peter for a moment and then looks away.

'Ha!' says George. 'You sleep with them and then you can move off! So what is there to mope about? Punch the head! The head!'

David looks up again. The sadness in his eyes is like a pane of shattered glass.

'Nothing. Nothing to mope about.'

He gets up and pushes past Peter. Then he opens the fridge, takes out a beer and sits down next to George.

The next few days with David are awful. Without Jeremiah, he seems to have lost his appetite for life.

'I found this book for you. It is poetry... David? You must eat. You haven't touched your *kapenta*. Eat and then we will go to a museum.'

'Leave me alone, Chipo. Please. Just go away.'

Then one night he went out with Peter. He didn't want to. All he wanted to do, he said, was sleep.

'You can't sleep day and night like some sick woman. Get up!' Peter threw David's jacket at him.

David went out without even brushing his teeth or combing his hair. When they came back several hours later, past three o'clock, they were not alone.

I heard the giggling as they opened the front door.

'This, girls, is where we live.'

I fumbled for my glasses as Peter flipped on the light.

'Who is *she*?' one of the women asked, pointing a long pink fingernail at me sitting up in bed in my nightdress.

'Hmm, oh, that is just our friend's little sister. Ignore her.'

'Come, let's dance!' Peter turned on the radio and the two women began to dance with him. They looked bored as they moved, slowly and mechanically. One of the women was wearing a tight red dress that only just covered her modesty. It kept on rising up her thighs as she moved, but she did not seem to notice or care.

'David? David! Get our lovely guests something to drink.'

David stood in the doorway. He was the last in. He could barely walk, he was so drunk. In his hand was a Bacardi Breezer. He staggered into the room and sat down on his mattress with his head between his legs.

Peter and the two women were still dancing. One of the women took out her cellphone and started to take pictures of Peter and the other woman, who made ridiculous poses. The women were not Zimbabwean, that was for sure. Not with dresses like that and all that gold jewellery. They looked like the sort of women who spent their time in the Long Street bars waiting for tourists to buy them a drink.

I pulled the blanket up to cover myself and tried to get David's attention.

'David, are you all right?'

His head swung up and he looked at me uncomprehendingly. Then he closed his eyes and nodded. Raising his bottle, he saluted me and took another gulp before letting the empty bottle drop.

'Dave-ed,' crooned the woman taking the photos, 'come and dance with us.'

She tottered over in her high heels and helped him to his feet. David went with her, but, rather than dancing, he stood swaying in one spot, his eyes closed, his mouth open, as the woman, her arms now around his neck, giggled like a teenager.

I couldn't look.

Suddenly there was a shriek of outrage and disgust. The women were angry. They had stopped dancing and were swearing in a language I couldn't understand. David had been sick on one of the women's shoes. Secretly I felt pleased. A woman like her had no right to a man like David, even if he was an *ngochani*.

The women went to the door, shouting their disgust at the two brothers. The one whose shoes had been soiled took a dishcloth from the table and wiped her shoes down before throwing the cloth at David.

'Wait!' cried Peter after them. 'Look what you have done now!' he said to David as he followed the women down the corridor. 'Leaticia, Alice – wait!'

I got out of bed and closed the front door. David was on his hands and knees in front of the pool of vomit. I picked up the dishcloth that the woman had used to clean her shoes. Going into the bathroom, I rinsed it under the tap and filled a bucket with some Jik and hot water. When I got back to the room, David hadn't moved. I went down on my knees, too, and began to clean the vomit off the carpet.

'Don't worry, David. Everything will be all right.'

'Please, Chipo,' David said, his head bowed low, 'please leave me alone.'

My cellphone beeps. I look at it. Another message. The third today. I move away from Jean-Paul so he can't see what it says.

Phone 0823563442

It is Doctor Ongani's number. I delete this message as I had deleted the previous ones. A half-hour later, another. Jean-Paul raises his eyebrows.

'Everything OK, Chipo?'

'Yes. It's just George.'

Chipo, I would STILL like to speak with you. Dr Ongani.

Eventually he will tire of contacting me. That is what I tell myself. I turn off the cellphone and put it in my bra. I do not want to see him again. I do not want David to fall in love with me. Not like this. I begin to iron again. To press the hot nose of the iron down. Only work can distract me. I fear being left with my guilty thoughts. I know what I have done. I have betrayed David. *Ngochani* or not, I have betrayed him. I can feel Mama's spirit looking down. She is ashamed.

He will go away, Chipo. David will get better and no one will ever know. You are safe.

Two days later. A knocking at the door. I open it. Doctor Ongani has found me. But how?

'You are a very difficult young woman to get hold of. You haven't been replying to my SMSes. Or taking my phone calls. Not very nice, after all I have done to help you. I suppose your cellphone is out of order?' The Doctor tuts like I am a naughty child.

He takes off his black hat and hands it to me, together with his cane with its carved top. The carved top is of a face covering its eyes with its hands. Doctor Ongani has told me that he carved it himself. I do not know why, but even when I saw that walking stick in his office, I had not liked looking at it. Reluctantly, I take it and the hat as the Doctor walks past me into the flat.

'Chipo, Chipo. You are not a woman of your word. Have you forgotten that you still owe me a sum of money?' He looks around him, surveying the room and the furniture, but his expression does not reveal what he thinks of our home.

I am too terrified to do anything but shake my head. At least everyone else is out.

'Sit down. I have a proposition.'

Without speaking a word, I sit.

When George gets home, he finds Doctor Ongani and me still sitting at the kitchen table. I feel sick to my stomach when I see George. I know he will be angry that he has come home to find a stranger in our flat. I want to disappear. Please, God, let me disappear. I close my eyes and open them again. But I am still in the room. And Doctor Ongani is still there too. There is no escape.

'Who the hell is this, Chipo?'

'Ah, you must be George. Doctor Ongani. Pleased to make your acquaintance. Your sister and I have been waiting for you.'

George shakes Doctor Ongani's hand reluctantly and looks at me as if to say, *What shit have you got us into now, Tortoise?* Then he turns his attention to the Doctor.

'You are not Zimbabwean?'

Doctor Ongani shakes his head.

'And not South African. So where are you from? I cannot place your accent.'

'From here, from there. What does it matter? Please, sit. Your sister and I have a business proposition.'

As Doctor Ongani is on his way out, David arrives home. I have no idea where he has been. None of us does. He stinks of cigarette smoke. He looks at Doctor Ongani, puzzled.

George introduces them. 'This is one of our roommates – David.'

'Ah, David.' Doctor Ongani greets him with a firm handshake, but all along he has his eyes on me. He had already told me what he would do if I didn't cooperate: 'I think David would be *most* upset if he found out that *you* were the reason for his friend's disappearance. Who knows what he might do? A betrayal like that...' He whistled slowly through his teeth.

Letting go of David's hand, Doctor Ongani scrunches up his face. 'You look... somehow familiar. Have we met?'

David shakes his head. 'Not to my knowledge, *baba*.'

He looks awful these days. His shirt is dirty but he doesn't seem to care or notice. If I offer to wash it, he brushes me off.

Doctor Ongani keeps his gaze on me. I close my eyes. In my mind I see his carved cane top. No hope, Chipo. No hope.

When I open my eyes again, Doctor Ongani is smiling. 'You are certain? It must be my mistake, David. *Sincere* apologies.'

That evening, we discussed Doctor Ongani's proposition. Here was an opportunity, George said, to make serious rand before the World Cup deadline. Here was the chance we had been praying for to really prosper and be in a position to do something if the rumours proved true.

But David was adamant. He wanted no part. He was like the old David.

'Well, I told Doctor Ongani it is either all of us or none of us, so I will have to call him.'

But Doctor Ongani wasn't about to let his golden goose fly away as easily as that. When a disappointed George phoned and told him we couldn't proceed because David wouldn't agree, the Doctor asked George to pass the phone to David. I don't know what he said to him, but David agreed to meet the Doctor down on Long Street. He was gone for more than two hours.

When David returns to the flat with Doctor Ongani, his expression is completely different. He can't bring himself to make eye contact with us. He looks like a boy who has been caught cheating on his maths test and is being hauled up before his classmates.

'Good news, my friends,' Doctor Ongani announces as he steps through the door. 'David and I have spoken and he has had a change of heart.'

We all look at David. None of us can believe it.

'David?' George asks. 'Is this true?'

David keeps his eyes on the ground as he speaks.

'I have listened to Doctor Ongani's proposition...' A pause. 'And I have decided...' Another pause. David can't get the words out. Doctor Ongani reaches forward and puts his hand on David's shoulder.

'He has decided that it is not such a terrible proposition after all.'

David bites his lip and nods.

'So all is settled,' Doctor Ongani says. He sits himself down at the kitchen table. No one has invited him to do so but that doesn't seem to bother him. He helps himself to a glass of Stoney's and smacks his lips.

'And Chipo?' George asks, turning to me. 'Are *you* sure?'

'I want to do it,' I tell my brother, hardly above a whisper. 'I want to. And then I want to go home.'

Home is a deep word. A parched throat. Happy is funny. It tastes like boiled sweets. Sad is grey. Like stale *foufou* or flat beer. Love? Love is bittersweet. A ripe, bright orange and its sharp zest. Hope. Hope is a big word. It tastes like meat and pap. If you are not careful, it can get caught in your throat and you will choke.

Later on, when the scheme is just starting to take shape, I ask Doctor Ongani what he said to David to change his mind.

The Doctor and I are alone in the flat. All the others are out at the post office photocopying flyers for our new business.

At first he does not answer. 'Oh,' he says, 'I can be very persuasive.'

He picks up the mug that he has just drained of its tea and indicates with a nod that I am to fill it for him again.

I do as he asks and watch him sip it slowly. Then he sets it down and strokes his beard. 'You see, Chipo, secrets are really very nasty things. They can get us into all sorts of trouble, especially if we want our secrets to stay secret. Some people will do almost anything.'

Suddenly I feel a cold shudder of fear.

'You didn't tell David about me and you? You didn't tell him about the letter? You promised…'

'Oh, no no, Chipo. You and I have an agreement.' Doctor Ongani smiles and brushes my concerns aside. 'Naturally, he wanted to know how I knew about his *preferences*… I explained that that is my job. To know what nobody else does. But not to worry, I told him, I can be discreet. But of course discretion comes at a price, and that price was his cooperation.'

'Was he angry?'

'At first. But he is not stupid, your David. A bright young man. Just think, I told him, with all the money you make you will be able to go and look for your Jeremiah. Together you will be able to go and study, get good jobs, live as you please. Life is so much easier when you are part of the successful middle classes, so much more... *liberal*.'

Suddenly the Doctor puts up his hand for me to be silent and still. I freeze. Has someone overheard us? As swift as a cobra, his hand shoots out and grabs a mouse that I haven't even noticed had been nibbling at some breadcrumbs at our feet. Doctor Ongani drops the mouse into my empty glass and puts his hand over the top so that it can't jump out. He holds it up to the light. Together we silently examine the mouse scrambling and trying to climb the sides of the glass.

'You see,' Doctor Ongani says, standing up and walking to the open window, 'this will be a situation that profits everyone. Think, with the money you could get some nice mousetraps, Chipo. Terrible creatures, mice and rats. Spreaders of disease.' With this, he tips the glass and lets the mouse fall the seven storeys.

Sixteen

From the slow, deliberate way Doctor Ongani takes off his hat and puts it on the table at his next visit, I know his plans have taken a fresh turn.

'We should run our business from President's Heights for practical reasons.'

He says he has found a room to rent down the corridor. It gives me goose bumps to think of him living just a few doors down, but I try to console myself. Just do as he asks. It will be over soon. Then you will all have enough money to go home and live well. Soon this will all be behind you. This is what Doctor Ongani has promised.

But with each passing day, Doctor Ongani grows closer, not farther away. He arrives with a suitcase. Inside are three suits, all black, that he tells me to brush.

'They got dusty with the workmen.'

And I must polish the wooden top of his cane.

Very quickly, he lays down the law. I am not allowed to talk to, or even see, the customers. I must remain an enigma. My job will be to sit with the *muti* behind the purple curtain. The customers will be able to see my outline so that they can be assured I am there. As far as the customers are concerned, I will be working my magic on the *muti*. And Jean-Paul? What about my job with him?

'You will have to give it up. You are my assistant now.'

Within a day of moving next door, he has put up a large sign: 'Doctor Ongani and Real Live Albino – Special Extra Powerful *Muti* to Improve Your Luck.' George, Peter and David are dispatched with new flyers to slip under the doors of all the flats and to hand out in the surrounding streets. Before he takes his share of flyers, David looks at me sadly. Is there no turning back?

No. There is not. Even though business is slow at first. There is plenty of competition. Long Street has many who make grand promises. Tourist offices with pictures of lions, leopards, elephants and giraffes, all waiting, they claim, to be photographed by you. Bars – three for one every happy hour. Best hamburgers in Cape Town. Young women promising to make a man feel like a king for a night for a hundred or two hundred rand. Want to eat alligator and buck meat but drink ice-cold Castle beer and use a toilet that can flush? Well, at Mama Afrika you can! Also psychics. *Sangomas* or spiritual healers famous for their ability to call upon the power of the ancestors and promising cures for all sorts of maladies.

If you turn off Long Street onto the cobbled Church Street, where the antique dealers sell their pretty trinkets from cloth-covered tables, and proceed on to Greenmarket Square, young women will offer you blue and white flyers that read:

DOCTOR ELIJAH.
FORTUNE TELLER. PALM READER &
TRADITIONAL & SPIRITUAL HEALER. SOLVING:

Financial problems
Re-unite Lovers

Family Matters
Win Court Cases
Business problems
Re Connect to Your Ancestors
Removal of Witch Crafts
Mental Illness
Reveals Lovers Future
Fixing Immoral Spouses
Bare-ness (Lack of children)
Removing Bad Luck
For seeing Evil Spirits

I do not know how we can compete with such promises. But Doctor Ongani is not worried.

'Hasn't got an albino,' is all he says when George shows him our competitor's advertisement. He drops a chicken bone onto his plate and gestures that it is time for me to clear it.

He is right. Whatever Doctor Elijah's promises, those hungry for hope do come to our little room in President's Heights. First one. Then another. Then many.

A woman. I can see her petite outline. I sit behind my curtain among the buckets and jars of dried herbs, bones and animal parts.

'Sometimes I say to myself, you know what, you are a failure. Thirty years of age and what-what. You are *still* a maid. No better than your sister back in Malawi. Sure, I know that I am still beautiful, but for how much longer? Look. Already you can see, Doctor, this greyness to my skin that marks all women who are getting older. You can see it, Doctor?'

Doctor Ongani mutters something.

'What have I to show for my life in this country? I find myself looking at my Ma'am's daughter. She has just finished university. She has got a proper job with a briefcase and a motor car. She is only twenty-three. And that is why I am here, Doctor Ongani. I want that. Can you give me that? Can she, the *biri*, give me that?'

'Pssst. Have you heard about what's going on in President's Heights?'

'The white one?'

'Yes. The *ndundu*.'

'The—'

'Magical.'

'They say she can see in the dark.'

'That she can make any charm.'

'You know what they say.'

'How back home they bring them out to find…'

'… the bodies of drowned fishermen…'

'The gold and diamonds hiding in the earth.'

'Floor seven.'

'Look for the sign that says DOCTOR ONGANI. He is her keeper.'

I do not know what becomes of the woman who wants a job that requires a briefcase. But three immigrants in President's Heights found jobs in one week, one at a backpackers, where previously the manager had said no, he refuses, she must be able to speak Xhosa. For someone else, a family's residence documents came through. A young woman from Uganda lost her job, but two weeks later got some good news. A miracle had indeed occurred.

'The woman has a daughter with a new baby. She lives in Joburg. Together they have agreed that I should go work for her and help look after the child. So you see, Doctor, I have been saved.'

Now she will also be close to her brother and sister, who are living in that city. She cried tears of gratitude and brought a pot of delicious spicy chicken and yam stew to the flat to say thank you to Doctor Ongani and his albino.

Another man comes. I remember that he too was waiting for an identity document. Had been waiting for almost three years.

'I am telling you, I have been to Home Affairs, you know, what, every week for two months, but this time there were no delays. They did not say come back, come back, come back.'

A miracle! The documents were waiting.

'The man at the desk even smiled and called me brother. Thank you, Doctor!'

The woman from Uganda and the man from Mozambique both swore they would spread the word. Maybe some of the others did too.

'It is the one upstairs.'

'That one of the white skin.'

'She is the one who is responsible. Go to her.'

'She can improve your bad luck.'

'She can help.'

'Look, this suit I am wearing. She touched it. Now I never take it off.'

'My child was born healthy after the doctors said it could not.'

'Now I have a job.'

'Go.'

'Go to her.'

'You know how those *namphweris* are. You know their special powers.'

'But you know,' Doctor Ongani says three and a half weeks later, as he eats another mouthful of cassava and gravy stew, brought to the room by another grateful immigrant from our building, 'poor immigrants and foreigners are one thing. But it is the soccer, this World Cup, that everyone is vuvuzela-ing about. That is where the real money is to be made...'

'But who needs an albino for that?' George interrupts, draining his mug of tea and lighting a cigarette.

Over the past few weeks, he has begun to turn to Doctor Ongani more and more for advice. I could see by the way he looked at him that he was fast coming to respect the Doctor for his business sense. He had even agreed to allow the Doctor to take charge of the money.

'Why should he be in charge of the money?' Peter had his reservations. 'I don't like it.'

'This business was his idea. You heard what he said. Each week we will receive our share of the profits, as promised. If one week he fails to give it to us, then we will make sure he is sorry.'

No one addresses me directly. As usual, I am not a part of the negotiations. I sit in the corner knitting. Jean-Paul has recently taught me how to do it. I am cold in the room and think maybe I will make myself a scarf and, if I can manage it, some thicker socks. Day or night, my feet are as cold as ice in this forsaken building.

'I don't care how she was considered in Zimbabwe. But in many other African countries, including for some in this country, Chipo's condition represents luck. And everyone needs luck, my friend. The soccer player, the club manager, the fans. But do you know who needs luck most of all…?' Doctor Ongani pauses.

'Well, don't make us wait for you to shit it out, Ongani.'

Doctor Ongani frowns. 'The gambler, my dear George, the gambler. And the gambler is more desperate than even the poorest immigrant. The gambler is addicted to his gambling and to the quest to improve his luck.'

Later that night, George, his appetite whetted by Doctor Ongani's latest promises, arrives home dragging what looks like a school chalkboard. It is past two o'clock.

'Where did you get that?' I ask.

'Don't ask me stupid questions unless you do not want an answer.'

The top of the board says LOLA'S. So he has stolen it from outside one of the bars.

With a wet cloth, he wipes away the specials of the day and cocktails at half price.

'This is so we can keep track of what is going on. The odds, the bets. We need to keep one step ahead if we are going to pull this off.'

'Pull what off?'

'Our riches. South African rand! British pounds! American dollars!'

'I do not want to take money from them. You know that I have no talent like they say. Doctor Ongani and I have been lucky up to now, that is all.'

'This is the first good thing that has happened to us in our lives. Don't ruin it.'

~

The next evening, Doctor Ongani gives us a lesson in the art of betting. Betting for soccer matches is complicated, he explains. There are lots of different ways to do it. For example, there is what is called a simple bet on which team you think will win. But the men who run the betting shops are not stupid. That is not where the real fortunes rest. The real fortunes are to be made if you can predict the *details*. For example, which player on which team will score the first goal and at what time precisely. Or who will be the first to be swapped out on the pitch. There are other bets for the more adventurous. How many cans of Coca-Cola will be sold by such and such a vendor? How many boerewors rolls eaten from his stall? After how many minutes will the ladies' toilets run completely out of toilet paper?

'It is in the details, my friends, that the gamblers' fortunes are made.'

Winter arrives, and with it the World Cup tourists. I can see them down on Long Street, pale and rowdy, excited by their team's prospects.

'The eighth of June 2010. Three days until the start of the World Cup,' George announces, looking at the calendar. 'Twenty-eight days left to make our fortune.' He puts down his pen and flops onto his mattress.

David is sitting where he spends every day: looking out of the window while drinking beer from one-litre bottles. I know that look.

Doctor Ongani comes in. He is carrying the chalkboard with a name written on it.

'What is *that*?' George asks.

'Our new company name, my friends. Fortune for the Unfortunate. What do you think?'

My brother shakes his head. 'Sounds like shit, Doctor. No disrespect. What about Gangster Paradise?'

'Too aggressive. We want to appeal to the ladies too, you know, George.'

A moment of reflective silence.

'Gamblers' Paradise.' It is David who says this. He is clearly drunk.

My brother pulls a face like he feels sick, but Doctor Ongani ponders the suggestion.

'No, no...' He snaps his fingers, indicating that Peter is to wipe away the previous name and replace it with this one. 'Gamblers' Paradise... It is short. Direct. Perhaps a little sentimental, but sincere. A show of hands? Only George, Peter and Doctor Ongani raise theirs. David walks out and I do nothing.

'Three yes, two abstentions. Democracy has spoken. Gamblers' Paradise it is. Ah, I feel like a member of South Africa's great Parliament.'

'There is something else,' George says. He unfolds a chart. A soccer chart. It came free in the *Cape Argus* a couple of weeks ago, he explains.

'If we are going to succeed we need to keep track of who is winning, who is losing, the scores, which players are delivering the goods.'

'Good thinking, my friend! Excellent!' Doctor Ongani runs his fingers over the paper poster as my brother pins it to the wall with some brass pins he has bought.

'There, now we are ready! But first,' Doctor Ongani says, 'on this auspicious day, I think we can afford to order some Nando's peri-peri chicken. Two family meals please, Peter.'

Afterwards, wiping his greasy fingers, George reads to us from the match calendar.

'OK, there are eight groups, four teams per group. Group A is South Africa, France, Mexico, Uruguay. Group B is Argentina, Greece, Nigeria, South Korea. Group D...'

As George continues, I catch sight of Jean-Paul leaving his room to go to the toilet. He stops and listens. Then, catching my eye, he shakes his head slowly. I had told him that I would not be able to help him like before because my brother needed my help. I couldn't tell him the truth, but I know that Jean-Paul senses that the constant presence of Doctor Ongani means mischief is afoot.

Today, 9 June, the government has asked everyone to blow their vuvuzelas at precisely twelve noon to show their support for the World Cup and South Africa's soccer team, Bafana Bafana. At noon I stand by the window to see if people will do it. And they do. As the clock hands reach twelve, cars slow down and the passengers blow through their open windows. Workers and customers come out of shops and restaurants to stand on the pavement and blow their red, green, blue and yellow vuvuzelas non-stop like they are trying to blow down the walls of Jericho. The locals are blowing hardest of all.

All the blowing makes such a racket that Jean-Paul covers his ears.

'Too much noise,' he complains when I go to his room. I can see it sets his nerves on edge.

Doctor Ongani is out. From Jean-Paul's window, I can see George and David standing down in the street, too. But they aren't blowing. George has his arms folded and David just stares ahead like one of those zombies whose brains have been eaten in George's Nollywood films. No one blows a thing in our building except maybe their noses. We know this World Cup does not belong to us. No amount of government what-what can convince us otherwise. Afterwards, when everyone has gone back inside, there is a feeling on the street like it's a festival day. But the mood in President's Heights remains heavy. Inside, we foreigners are still racking our brains to think of how we can raise enough rand before the 11 July deadline. We've got four weeks, one month, thirty-one days. The opening of the World Cup will start the clock ticking. If I stand and close my eyes, I can feel all that worry and concern seeping in through the walls and up through the linoleum and the carpets, like the smell of boiling fish. Come 11 July, who knows where we will be? Is every passing day bringing us closer to our deaths, or will we escape with our goods?

I go back to Jean-Paul. He is sewing at his machine for hours at a stretch. Maybe he too is worried, even though he doesn't want to admit it. I pick up another pair of trousers and continue the ironing I had started. I still help him when I can. Making the pile of altered dresses and trousers smooth and perfect will help soothe my nerves, I tell myself. There is still time, Chipo. Still hope. But my heart feels like I have opened a bag of rice to find maggots feasting inside.

Our first betting customer is a gambler and he is certainly desperate. A coloured man with tattoos like dark blue spider webs spun up his arms and across his hands. The tattoos, I am told after he leaves, that is normal. But the two fingers missing from his right hand… these are another matter. He owes money and he owes it to the sort of people who don't extend their credit, he tells us. He is already two months late. And for every month they chop off a finger.

'I'd drink *hondepis*,' he explains, 'if I thought it would work, and so far I have done everything, even eaten cooked vulture brains from one of those fokken *sangomas* in Khayelitsha because he said it'd help me to see the future so I could predict results, and fokkol. But if my luck doesn't change soon, well, I won't be seeing the finals, if you know what I mean. And if I do, I won't be able to wipe my own *gat*.'

This gambling man is looking at me and he is waiting.

'So, which game would you like her to influence?' George asks. He is doing his best to sound calm, confident, even wearing Peter's green suit that is one size too big.

'Bafana Bafana versus Uruguay.'

'So you want Uruguay to lose…?'

'What? No, fok… What has this country ever done for me? No way. I want Uruguay to win.'

'To win?' My brother can't hold his tongue. 'But they have been playing like blind goats. Uruguay, shit! They couldn't even beat the French, and *they* at the moment have no power, no skill! They only qualified because Henry put the ball into the goal with his hand and then denied it…'

The man shrugs. 'That's not my problem. That's *your* problem. The bookies all have Bafana Bafana to win. The only way I can make enough money is if the other team does it.'

He points his finger at me sitting in the back.

'You make South Africa lose, *wit kaffir*, you hear me? I don't care what voodoo you have to do. If you don't, I'll come back here and you'll lose more than just your fingers, *verstaan?*'

I open my mouth. No words come out. I want to say that I am sorry, that I do not possess the power to help him. I want to say many things. Instead I say nothing.

'Be calm, sir,' says Doctor Ongani. 'We will take care of it. Or your money back.' Doctor Ongani is calm. He is used to this. But I can tell by how my brother swallows and shuffles in Peter's too-big suit that he is scared.

I am scared too. Bafana Bafana lose? Everyone knows they are the favourites. Perhaps George, like me, is wondering whether we have all bitten off more than we can swallow. This coloured is not some immigrant like us. If things go wrong, what then? Will we be reported to the police and deported? It is a big risk. Do Doctor Ongani and my brother really know what they are doing?

The man is not yet satisfied. He turns to me. My job is simply to be in the back. Supposedly I am doing something to the *muti*. But I am not allowed to speak. The customers seem satisfied just to see my outline there. Near the jars of dried herbs and bits of bone and fur.

'Will she go in the night and bewitch all the other team, make it so their legs wobble like water and they cannot kick the ball and all that other voodoo kak that you darkies do?'

Doctor Ongani puts his hand on the man's shoulder. 'She will do it, my friend. She will fix it so that the South Africans play like fools. Now go home.'

When the man has left, Doctor Ongani turns to face all of us. 'Do not worry, keep your heads. Everything will be all right.'

'Chipo?'

'Yes, Mama.'

'Is the window open?'

'No, Mama.'

'I'm so cold. Can you find me another blanket?'

~

Eight-thirty in the evening. Long Street. Cape Town. Wednesday, 16 June. First round. South Africa versus Uruguay. We are all crowded into our flat. George has knocked off work but is still in his restaurant uniform. For once, few eyes are on me. Instead, they are on the men entering the pitch at the Loftus Versfeld Stadium in Pretoria. Vuvuzelas blowing. An angry hornet's nest. National anthems. First Uruguay. Then South Africa. The children who have accompanied the players onto the pitch leave the field. The players all shake hands. Like the hearts of the players themselves, with every passing minute my heart is beating faster and faster.

I am on the pitch too. On the grass. Smelling the freshly mowed earth. I am in the players' straining muscles and their pounding hearts. And I am in the ball. The new Jabulani ball. On the turf. Inside the referee's silver whistle. I make him itch to pull out his yellow and red cards. Under my breath I speak to Mama's spirit. Please, Mama. Help us.

A lot depends on this, Doctor Ongani has said. If the word spreads that we were somehow able to influence the coloured man's luck, then we would have more customers than we would know what to do with. Then, sooner than we all know, we will have the money to return home, search for proper houses, open tuck shops in a more reputable market, or even cafés. Whatever we want. Money enough so that all four of us can go elsewhere. George and I back to Zimbabwe. The brothers to Paris, London, even New York. And Doctor Ongani? He says he hasn't yet decided. All of this before 11 July and the deadline our hosts have imposed upon us. Isn't that, after all, what they say they want? To get rid of us? I am exhausted. Tired of worrying. I look at the South African players. It is only a game, I tell myself. So what if the other team wins and South Africa loses? Who would it hurt? I take a deep breath, close my eyes and inside my head I scream, LOSE!

After Uruguay defeats South Africa 3–0, word quickly spreads. From one dark and overcrowded flat in President's Heights to the next and up and down Long Street and beyond, to the immigrant communities of Woodstock, Observatory and Wynberg. And some locals too. Soon there are many others all desperate to pay the albino to influence the soccer outcome and their bank balances. Doctor Ongani and George are so pleased that they do not even mind that our business attracts the interest of some more unsavoury Long Street characters.

After George comes home one evening after a night on the town, Doctor Ongani tells him the news.

'The Tanzanians from floor three have contacted me. They want a meeting.'

I have heard about these Tanzanians before. They are known as local drug dealers and are said to enjoy impunity from the police, whom they bribe. What are Doctor Ongani and George doing getting involved with people like these? But George is hardly listening. He is patting his pockets.

'My cellphone…'

'Of course, I expected it…'

'Shit, it's gone. My cellphone has been stolen. Hello, my cellphone has been stolen. Does anyone care?'

'Can't be helped, I suppose,' Doctor Ongani says with a sigh. 'Price of success.' He picks up his cellphone and dials a number. 'Hello, Julius? Doctor Ongani here. Yes, yes. Time to arrange a meeting.'

Seventeen

I have often imagined the day I would say goodbye to George and start out on my own. I would leave a letter on the table, propped against the bag of mealie meal. In the letter I would thank him, of course, for taking care of me for so many years. I would try not to hold the insults and names against him. I would wish him well and promise to be in touch. What then? My first steps on my own. I would take my umbrella, my sunblock cream, my spectacles. Now I own the clothes from Jean-Paul too. The dresses with jackets that he made for me in the fabrics I had chosen myself at Fabric City. What else? What else belongs to me? I do not have a photo of Mama. She never liked to have her photograph taken. Would turn away from the camera.

'What do you want a photograph for?' she would ask. 'Photographs cause your memory to go lax because you think, ah, now there's a photograph to take memory's place.'

By the time she was sick, it was too late for photos. I didn't want to remember her like that. And now? Now I use my eyes like the shutter of a camera. The eyelids snap down. Remember this moment, Chipo. And this. It will be over soon, do not forget.

'Do not forget me.' Mama's words towards the end.

Of course, some things you want to forget. Some photos we would rather burn. But the brain has its way of hanging on. Of not letting moments pass into oblivion. 'Time heals all wounds.' That is what Mama once said. But does it?

A banging on the door. Impatient fists on wood.

'The Tanzanians,' my brother hisses.

Doctor Ongani stands up to straighten his suit and smooth his tie. He picks up his walking stick and grips it tightly.

'Let them in.'

David and Peter do not look pleased, but they say nothing. They wanted, I know, nothing to do with the Tanzanians, but my brother convinced them that this was our chance to make an important business connection.

We have something the Tanzanians want and they are willing to negotiate. Lucky it is not the other way round. Since Uruguay defeated South Africa we have sometimes up to ten customers a day asking us to improve their betting luck. And each day this number is growing.

'Things have been going so well with your soccer fortune-telling and the gamblers that they are willing to speak with us as equals. Partners, not passengers. And there are benefits, Chipo, police protection…' said Doctor Ongani.

'She has no brain for business,' my brother interrupted. 'Just do what we tell you, OK, Tortoise?'

'Is this her? Is she the one who influenced the match so that that bullshit Uruguay won three to zero?'

'It was her, Julius,' Doctor Ongani affirms, 'combined with my skills.' He indicates that the four men in jeans, silk shirts and sunglasses should sit down. They make themselves comfortable on the plastic chairs, leaving the others to stand. My brother fiddles with the pack of matches in his pocket, but keeps his face steady. He is excited, and I know that if he could he would be grinning from ear to ear. For the first time since arriving in South Africa, he has something that other people actually want. This is his big chance.

It is agreed. Fifteen per cent to Julius and the Tanzanians, and they will make sure that we are not robbed and that the police leave us alone. They will also spread the word among the illegal betters and gamblers. They know where the men and women who just can't help themselves spend their time.

'This could be a situation that works out for all of us. Believing that they have more luck on their side, gamblers will be inspired to take more daring risks. The gambler-shop men will benefit, Julius and his friends will benefit and you will benefit,' Doctor Ongani says as he, David, Peter and George gather around the table waiting for me to finish making dinner.

Doctor Ongani smiles. As they were leaving, one Tanzanian, the man Ongani had referred to as Julius, turned to me and said: 'Very lucky for those searching in the mines. Back home I could sell you by the kilo!'

Julius poked his finger into my arm. Then he tossed his head back and laughed.

Saturday 19 June. Last night Germany lost 0–1 to Serbia and all around there are rumours. Is this coincidence? Or the Curse of the Dark Continent? Or is some sort of other African magic afoot? This morning is surprisingly quiet. Many of the foreign fans are in shock about their team's bad run of luck. Across the city, there is much grumbling among the Germans as they crack the tops of their boiled eggs and eat their cheese and ham. The French dip their croissants in silence in hotel and guesthouse breakfast rooms. A loss against Ghana! A draw with the Ivory Coast! A narrow victory over Cameroon! It is like a nightmare. What is going on in this accursed country? On this dark continent? They have never known anything like it before. There is talk of African black magic at work. Definitely voodoo. African witchcraft. They are sure of it.

The previous evening, the Long Street bars were quiet as the German fans walked home, their flags draped over their shoulders like cloaks of despair. The mood on the streets was in stark contrast to the mood in our flat. George and Doctor Ongani celebrated another success with fried chicken and bottles of Castle. They had encouraged everyone to support underdog Serbia, claiming I would help them to play like gods. More happy customers meant more profits for us.

In his room I can hear the whirr of Jean-Paul's sewing machine. These days, without my help, he often works far into the night on his creations. I miss helping him with his deliveries. But now I am needed behind the curtain in Doctor Ongani's room at all times.

'Do you think Jean-Paul is all right?'

'Who cares?' my brother hisses. He is admiring the new pair of sunglasses and Adidas sneakers he bought with the previous night's takings. He pulls a face, and then bursts out laughing.

I decide to go and see Jean-Paul. Ever since the thing with Doctor Ongani started, I hardly see him.

'I thought you might like a slice of cake? It's banana and mango. Very good,' I say, standing in the doorway.

Jean-Paul stops what he is doing and looks up at me. His mouth is full of pins. His eyes narrow. Then he pushes a chair up and indicates that I am to sit down.

As I sit, Jean-Paul does not speak to me. He pretends to be working on a suit jacket, but all the time his eyes are on me. Eventually I feel so uncomfortable that I stand up and make an excuse about needing to assist George. Jean-Paul does not seem surprised. He nods and watches me walk to the door.

'OK, here is the line-up. Group D, Ghana versus Australia. Best we can offer is a draw. Look at the match results to date… She is good but not a miracle worker. Yes, it's two hundred ZARS. It's the next round, so the prices have gone up.'

Behind the curtain, I slip into my own thoughts. Some of what I think about I would rather not. David is unable to work, I heard the Doctor. He is depressed and drinking too much. God, if I have any powers, help David get better. I didn't mean for it to go this way, I tell myself. I just wanted, I just wanted… David. Yes. Think of something else. The doctor is busy with another client. The tenth in a row today. What will this one want from me?

From behind the curtain I can see the shape of Doctor Ongani in his dark suit. He is wearing his hat. The other man, the customer, is tall and thin. He hardly speaks, but when he does I know he is not a foreigner like us. He is a local.

I can see that he is holding a piece of paper.

'Odds are five to one, my friend. So if you bet five hundred rand and win, you will still make two thousand three hundred rand profit. Not bad, hey?'

I need to go to the toilet. If Doctor Ongani does not give me a break soon… The man is silent. Sucks his teeth. Without another word, he leans forward. He is giving the money to Doctor Ongani.

'The *inkawu*?'

'Hmmm? Oh, yes. You can see her there. Through the curtain. She is silent, but in constant communication with the ancestors. Your money is as good as made.'

When the man has gone, Doctor Ongani opens his drawer and starts counting the day's takings so far. I pull back the curtain.

'I need to go to the toilet.'

The Doctor looks up from the bundle of blue hundred-rand notes for a moment.

'OK, quickly. We have another appointment in five minutes.'

I watch as he takes a few of the notes and stuffs them into a black pouch that he puts into the inside pocket of his jacket. The rest he locks in the bottom drawer of the desk.

'Do you know that now even tourists are coming to see Peter and I at the café? And others.'

'Who?' asks Doctor Ongani.

George lowers his voice. 'People in government. I think they are members of Parliament. They are worried about Bafana Bafana. They play France on Tuesday. Four o'clock.'

'Send them to me. But remember, make no promises.'

'There is a psychic octopus in Germany. They say it can predict the results.' George comes in holding a newspaper. He does this every morning before the first customer comes. I look at it with envy. I too want to know what is going on.

'Ha, ridiculous,' Doctor Ongani declares. 'What will those Germans think of next?'

'It has predicted the results perfectly so far. All I can say is that it is good for us that it is so far away.'

'George? I would like to see the newspaper.' But they do not hear me.

'No African would ever go to an octopus for results! They can say what they like, those journalists, it is not…'

'Yes, I know, it is not an albino.'

'George…'

'What *is* it, Chipo? Doctor Ongani and I are talking business here.'

'The newspaper. Couldn't you leave it here? I would so like to…'

'I need it now. I need to keep abreast with the teams' results. Maybe later I will bring it.'

But he never does.

'How much longer?'

'Chipo, how can you not trust me? You know your David is not well. He is not working. So the pressure is on to keep our home team fed.'

'Until the final. Your promise…'

'Yes, yes. Then I will go my way. And you can go yours. For me, I think London. I have always wanted to visit Buckingham Palace.'

I have no idea how much money we have made. I know we had customers. I saw their outlines and heard their voices through the curtain every day. So we are making money, yes. But I am worried. George is also spending. He arrived home one afternoon with a new iPod.

'You will like this, David. It records all the music digitally and stores it inside. Up to two thousand songs.'

'Only one problem, George. You need a laptop to put the music on it.'

'Ah, and what is this I have here in the other bag?'

'George, we are supposed to be saving to go home.'

'Oh, for goodness' sake… Don't trouble me, Chipo. What businessman doesn't have a laptop?'

What is the date? Whenever I try to ask George or Doctor Ongani, they just brush me off.

'Who cares?' they say. All I need to know is that it is Germany versus France or Netherlands versus Spain. That's all that matters.

But I think the 11 July deadline is approaching because more and more of our immigrant cousins are coming asking for our help.

'I am a student at university. The other students don't know I am from Zimbabwe. They think I am Xhosa, because you see, I can speak like them. My father was a Xhosa. I am not eligible for a bursary because of my foreigner status. I am having trouble meeting my tuition fees. I don't know what to do. And now these rumours for July.'

'It is my dreams, Doctor. Every night. Same dreams. I cannot get the sounds of killing and dying out of my head. My wife does not understand. She was in the forest. She hid. She does not know what they made us do. I cannot tell her. But the dreams. I must stop the dreams. Do you think we are in danger? Can she protect me?'

'Back home in Nigeria, those sorts of children, we call them witches. I myself never believed. But ever since my niece has come to stay, my son cannot breathe properly. The doctor says it is asthma. My niece is a quiet girl and my sister's child. But my husband is certain. She has put a curse on our son and she says we will all die soon at the hands of the locals.'

'Doctor, I don't know what to do.'

'We are at our wits' end.'

'I am losing weight.'

'Cannot eat.'

'There is blood in my piss.'

'My boss says I must find other work.'

'Three weeks' notice.'

'Can you...?'

'Can she...?'

'Can you and she help me, Doctor?'

These immigrants say they want some extra help. They want something to ensure their protection. George and Peter discuss this after one man from Tanzania leaves. I am sitting eating my supper under the window. George doesn't even know how to cook the beans properly. They are still a bit tough.

'We could give them, you know, like that man just asked, something *physical*.'

'Hmm, something she has touched?'

'Or something, you know, from her body.'

Both turn to look at me.

'Hold still, Chipo. Stop being such a baby. It will grow back. No one even sees you these days, anyway. You are behind the curtain... For God's sake, stop crying. I can't cut properly.'

∼

REAL ALBINO HAIR.

GET RID OF YOUR ENEMIES (150 ZARS AN ENVELOPE).

A dream. I am walking home. Walking back to Zimbabwe. The sky is blue, the sun not too intense. George is with me. The hills are green, thick and dense with forest. We are happy. There is a gentle slope and a path that leads through the vegetation. Birds are singing.

'Just a little bit further, Chipo,' he says. 'Soon we will be there.'

I try to follow George, but suddenly the path becomes very steep and narrow. Sunlight is shining in my eyes and I have forgotten my umbrella. George pushes on ahead.

'George!' I cry out, 'George!'

The path is too steep for me now and the soft greenery has been replaced by rocks and dry earth.

'George, where are you? I cannot keep up!'

But George has already disappeared.

Ever since Doctor Ongani has come into our lives, I can see how George regards himself. He no longer thinks General's ex-garden boy. Rather, he sees a man in a suit with two cellphones, a laptop and new Adidas sneakers. Other times he sees what, with his gold chains and baseball cap turned backwards? One of those American rap stars he so admires?

And David? David is a ghost of himself. I watch him from the window when he is out. I do not know if he is still working at the restaurant. Doctor Ongani said David lost his job. 'Always at the bottle these days.'

I have seen David leave President's Heights at ten in the morning, at three in the afternoon, sometimes as late as ten at night. I have heard him and Peter arguing down the corridor outside the flat. Glass smashing. Then fast footsteps, angry thudding ones, and slamming doors.

I do not need to cook any more, or go out and run errands. For my own safety it is thought better that I not leave this one room, not even to go back to the flat. I must sleep, eat and shit here, in the place where Doctor Ongani and I see his clients and he is now to take my place in the flat with David, George and Peter. In this, my new home, there is a desk with a chair, the curtained sections where I must stand with the *muti* when the Doctor is consulting and, in the corner, a bed and sink. I must stay here for my own safety, you see. Doctor Ongani says that now, even Julius and the Tanzanians consider me a most rare commodity and, given half a chance, given half a chance... What? I cannot remember what Doctor Ongani said. Or George. I watch their mouths move these days, but often I cannot attach a sense. When they lock me in from the outside at night, with only my memories and dreams for company, I am in the back of a truck going to a country I do not know. Leaving home. Home sounds like poem. Jeremiah used to like poetry.

'You are a gift,' Doctor Ongani often says. 'We must take care of you.'

Chipo. Gift. But Chipo also sounds like *chipko*, the Shona word for 'ghost'. Never forget, Chipo. Your name is... Every day that I am locked away, I feel myself fading, disappearing.

I miss. I miss the Mountain Dew Superette. The touch of sunlight, not first filtered by glass. The window in this room will not open. It has been nailed shut.

I close my eyes and try to remember David and me that day in the art gallery. Beauty in the eyes of the beholder. Beholder sounds like boulder. There is an invisible boulder keeping me here, I think to myself, as I wait for Peter or George to bring me my lunch. And Jean-Paul? What of him now? Why does he never come and visit? I miss the smell of coffee.

I breathe onto the window. My breath fogs the glass and I write. My name is Chipo. In Shona it means Gift. My name is. My name is. I blow over the glass again. This time I write:

CHIPO
GHOST
IM
PEST
O
K
O

I must ask for a pen and some paper.

'There is an article in the newspaper. The local *sangomas* are predicting the final result…'

'Let me see that.'

From behind the curtain, I watch Doctor Ongani's outline as he reaches forward to take the *Cape Times* from George.

Doctor Ongani reads out loud: '*Sangomas* predict African team will not win World Cup trophy.'

'What should we do?'

'Which African teams are left? Ghana and—?'

'Just Ghana…'

'Well, it is also a matter of odds. One African team left in the running against seven others.'

'So discourage bets on Ghana?'

'Correct. I will do the same... Except, George...'

My brother stands and waits for his orders.

'Except goals. We are willing to take payment for those wanting goals. Poor luck for the opponent teams. More power for the Ghana team, etc, etc. You and Peter know how it works by now. But no more wins. Understand?'

I watch George nod, turn and go.

'Chipo?'

I pull back the curtain. 'Yes, Doctor Ongani?'

'It is time for you to eat.'

Eighteen

'I know you. You are Chipo's tailor friend. From the Congo.'

Jean-Paul? What is he doing here?

'I am not from Congo. I am from Rwanda.'

Rwanda?

I sit behind the curtain. My head is swimming. Rwanda? Why has he never told me?

But he tells Doctor Ongani. Tells him everything while I am forced to listen. I scribble down notes. I want a record. Because I find I am forgetting things. My name is...

Here is some of what I managed to record:

Genocide 1994.

Village near the border with the Democratic Republic of the Congo.

Jean-Paul is a priest.

But sinful. Sleeping with a woman who lived in a neighbouring village. A member of his congregation. (I don't have time to get her name.)

He and mistress Hutu.

Wife a Tutsi (Marie).

Daughter, short and stocky like him, resembled the Hutu people too. At least in the eyes of the militia.

Militia sounds like fisher. What do they fish for? Human lives. Daughter spared when the militias came.

The neighbours must have protected his daughter too, because if the militia had discovered that she was the offspring of a marriage between Tutsi and Hutu, nothing could have saved her.

'And your wife?' Doctor Ongani asks.

'My wife?' A long pause. 'Chopped off her limbs, like sticks of sugar cane.' Marie murdered.

'Like a cockroach.'

And here is where words fail my friend. I stop scribbling. In my head I see Doctor Ongani wait for Jean-Paul to go on. He looks up at the clock. Half an hour already. He will be able to charge him extra. Jean-Paul has slumped forward. I hear the bang bang bang of him hitting his head rhythmically on the table, as though trying to knock the memory from it.

After a few seconds, he sits up. Sucks in air. Speaks again. My pen is ready.

His daughter's body was never found. He thinks. He knows. Swept over the border. With the tide of people fleeing.

'Refugees?' asks Doctor Ongani.

Refugees rhymes with fleas, I think to myself, biting my lip behind the curtain. Fleas know when to flee. Why has my friend come to us? What is he hoping for? I am starting to feel sick.

'No, no.' Jean-Paul shakes his head. 'Not the Tutsis. The Hutu militias fearing reprisals. I have prayed for fifteen years. I even spent some time in the camps of the DRC trying to find her.'

Fifteen. So I was three when he began. What can I remember of when I was three? Nothing. Mama would have had the tavern. George would have been six. The sound of a box of documents being emptied out onto the table. Letters. I see letters in my mind.

Hundreds and hundreds. All trying to locate the whereabouts of his daughter. He had written to them all, Jean-Paul says. The United Nations. The Red Cross. The Prime Minister of Britain. The President of France. Of Rwanda. The Pope at the Vatican. There were twenty-five letters addressed to the President of the United States. Bill Clinton, George Bush, even Obama. No one had helped. No one. Not even God. 'I have tried. Have prayed and prayed. He wants nothing more to do with me.'

So that's why he has come to us. Because his hope is bankrupt.

Nineteen

Can I, Chipo, see everything? The secrets of this world and of the next? Doctor Ongani says I can. He says I do not even need my spectacles any more, which is fortunate because they are broken. Doctor Ongani has been promising for weeks to replace my spectacles, but I am still waiting.

'You are special, Chipo. Gifted. You have special gifts.'

Of course I know that this is not really true. That I am just the same as I was before. But with each passing day, with each new promise I make to help someone, with each new bundle of hundred-ZAR notes Doctor Ongani takes, with each new success for our clients, even though I know it is – must be – just coincidence, I find myself getting more and more confused.

'You have special gifts, Chipo. Lucky for me that I was the one who found you.'

Sometimes when I am very tired I think I can see all sorts of things. For example, the blood swimming through my veins, beneath this pink skin of mine. It is red like All Gold tomato sauce, but thin like the ink of my biro before it ran out. I have asked for another pen, but Doctor Ongani has yet to bring it. I scratch what I can on this pad. Blood vessels. I can see the blood vessels too. How they carry the oxygen just like Mrs Guchu said, so that the heart and lungs and other organs can do their business. And not only my blood. I think I can see my food, too. If I stand in front of the mirror when Doctor Ongani has gone out, I can see the water I am drinking, sip by sip, then gulp by gulp, so that it spills down my chin and onto my blouse. Down down. It rushes down my throat, shimmering like spirits. And the food I am given. That they bring me.

No, I tell myself. You must not start to believe their lies. There is nothing magical about you. Nothing special. You cannot start to believe. If you do, then you will be lost. Lost for good, and there will be no way to find your way out once all of this is over. All these lies. All this deceit.

But will it ever end? I ask myself. Will Doctor Ongani ever let me go? He promised. Just remember who you are. Remember, Mama. Remember before.

But when I try to remember, all I can recall is Jean-Paul's face when Doctor Ongani took all his money. His face. Happy. Hopeful. That is how I imagined it. The termites burrowing in his heart, still for a moment. Even his deformed foot looked like it might blossom again. And why not? If I can do one, then why not the other? If I can bring them back together, then why not resurrect the dead?

Watch. This *sope* can turn water to wine. I drink another glass of water and wait for it to turn to wine in my mouth. Wine. Not beer. Not like the beer David now drinks when he should be at work. I sometimes believe I can see his thoughts. Right through this wall. I do not need to press my ear to the wall with a glass, loneliness driving me to do it, to hear something, anything of my old life. David. Beloved. My beloved. I am spared nothing. His thoughts creep under the door unrolling like secret messages, lovers' notes. But they sting like wasps.

He possesses an excellent memory, my David. It is his training as a lawyer. I knew it before. Now I can see it with my own eyes. Like that day. When George and Peter called Jean-Paul Buttock Beak. Something in David died at that moment. And other moments. I know it. A million other moments. Tiny heart attacks. I do not envy his good memory. Memory is my only company these days, but still there is much I would sooner forget.

Attack rhymes with smack. George only smacked me once. Across the face when I said I wanted to stop. That was how my spectacles broke. George has big hopes for the money I make. There are rumours. Rumours of cars and taxi businesses, and a house with a satellite dish.

Rumour sounds like tumour. That man who came last week. Tumour on his brain. Not a rumour. A fact. He was from Sudan. He brought the doctor's X-ray. Can your *sope* help with the tumour? he asked Doctor Ongani. Can she trick the demons and eat it away? Doctor Ongani nodded. She can. She can. She can.

Twenty

The World Cup final. Has it happened? What date is it? I want to know, but I have no one to ask. The streets are less crowded. The vuvuzelas are quiet. I have managed to find some Sellotape to bind my broken glasses, although I fear they will always be bent. I have stopped asking Doctor Ongani when my new spectacles will come.

'Spectacles are expensive, Chipo. And now that David has lost his job and George has quit, we have many people depending on us.' Obligations sounds like, sounds like, sounds like.

I watch the woman. It has been two weeks since last I saw her. I watch her walk with her dusters and flags. It gives me comfort to watch the same people. To observe their habits. Their lives are moving forwards while mine seems frozen, like those animals in their glass cages in the science museum.

Sometimes I think I hear fighting beyond the wall. Sometimes there is banging on this door. Then voices talking, whispering. Then nothing. When that happens I leave the window, get into bed, pull the blanket over my head and try not to be afraid. Doctor Ongani says we may have to move soon. That all sorts of jealous parties are conspiring against him. But he will keep me safe. Safe. Does it sound like chase? They are chasing. Who? Tell me?

'They who want what I have got, Chipo.'

Doctor Ongani looks tired. He has forgotten my pen again. I breathe onto the glass. Today is:

Monday   Thursday
Tuesday   Friday
Wednesday   Saturday?

I know today is not Sunday. The street would be quieter. So which? I decide today is Wednesday. I am alive. I write my crossword again:

CHIPO
GHOST
  IM
 PEST
  O   E
 KISS
  O   T

PLEASE DAVID. COME BACK.

And then one evening, when I least expect it, after Doctor Ongani has locked me into the room, David comes back to me. 'Chipo?'

'David? Is that you, David?'

'Yes, Chipo, can you hear me? Come to the door.'

I get up and press my ear to the wood.

'Listen, I have to be quick. I want to tell you that I am going to get you out of here, tonight. I am sorry, Chipo. I never should have agreed to all of this. It's gone too far, and now Doctor Ongani says, well, never mind what that bastard says. Listen, I have many things I need to tell you. Things I have not told anyone.'

'Me too, David.' My heart is beating hard and fast. It is so good to hear my friend again sounding like his old self. I realise how much I have missed him. 'There are things I need to tell you too. Things I am very sorry about. David, I—'

'We can talk about everything later, Chipo. Let's first get you away from here. I have to go. But I will come back for you tonight, when they are asleep. Be ready for me.'

'OK. Goodbye, David. Thank you.'

I listen to David walking down the corridor, whistling as if nothing has happened. For a long time I stand next to the door until I can't hear him any more. My heart continues to beat hard in my chest. I can't quite believe it. Can all that has been broken really be fixed? Can all that has gone crooked be set straight? I want to cry at this unexpected act of mercy. Will I be saved? Will I be saved by my David?

When darkness falls I lie on my bed, fully dressed. There are so many questions in my head that I hardly notice the hours pass. Is David really going to take me away? What has made him stop drinking? Isn't he worried about Doctor Ongani's blackmail? We will have to go. We can't stay here. All the others will be furious. Where will we go? What will he do when I tell him the truth about him and Jeremiah? Will he abandon me? I will have to take that chance.

At some point I drift off to sleep, only to be woken by blue lights bouncing against the walls and the howl of sirens on Long Street. A police raid. There hasn't been one for a while. I push my nose to the window but can't see where the commotion is. As I am trying to tilt my head to look down the street, I hear the thunder of boots running past my room. Voices. A banging next door. Orders being barked.

'Open up! It's the police!'

The sound of a wooden door bursting on its hinges. I am sure I can hear George's voice. Jean-Paul's too, shouting in French. And then David.

'Wait, I have nothing to do with them! Chiiipo!'

The shouting goes on for a long time, until eventually there is the sound of bodies struggling past the door.

'Chiiipo!'

David. It is David. His voice growing fainter as he is dragged further and further down the corridor.

And afterwards, silence. I lie awake the rest of the night, waiting for what, I do not know. I suppose I am waiting for David to come as he had promised, even though I know he won't come now. He can't. And in the morning it is the same. Silence. Stillness. No one comes to unlock my door. Not David. Not Doctor Ongani with my breakfast of mealie porridge. I am alone.

Two days later. Late afternoon and I am getting very hungry. It is strange to look down on so many restaurants and have no food myself. I try not to panic, even though sometimes I feel worry wiggling like a thousand earthworms inside me. When we were planting seeds in our garden, Mama said worms are a good sign. A sign that the soil is healthy. Worm shit makes plants grow big. I close my eyes and imagine picking the worms out of my stomach and brain one by one. I tell myself, once Doctor Ongani left you alone for three whole days, Chipo. Of course, then Peter brought me food. That was before Doctor Ongani said I was only to take food given by him.

'To some, you are more valuable dead than alive. They will stop at nothing. Even poison.'

Even if they have been arrested, surely they will not forget about me? Surely they will tell someone about Chipo, locked alone in this room without food? Of course, then they will have to confess everything. Tell the police the whole truth. But I am sure they will not let me starve to save their own necks. David. David will never let me starve. He will tell the police. Tell them to come and fetch me. I try to comfort myself with these and other thoughts.

My stomach rumbles. I have already gone through all the drawers in Doctor Ongani's desk but found nothing but small brown envelopes. He puts the *muti* in those. There was a time he wrapped his *muti* in newspaper and with pages torn from magazines. I liked that because then I had something to read. I would sit on the floor and page through. I would remember the General's wife.

There were no Choice Assorted Biscuits for me. No houseboy to bring me mango juice, either. Once, when Doctor Ongani forgot to bring me supper, I found a box of Cadbury's Dairy Milk chocolates that a grateful customer must have brought. I had eaten those lying on the floor, letting each morsel melt on my tongue as the room grew dark. I did not bother to turn on the light. Outside, the bars and their electric signs cast their own colours onto me. Red. Green. Blue. And for a while I felt better. If I had known I might be deprived of food again, I would have saved some. The ones with nuts inside.

I go and look at the boxes, jars and plastic buckets of *muti*. I do not like looking at the medicines, even when I had to sit behind the curtain when the patients and customers were there. But I am feeling very hungry. For a moment, I think there might be something to eat. I pick up a bunch of herbs and, after sniffing it, tear off some leaves. There are people who came to the Doctor to lose weight, others because they were growing thinner and thinner and couldn't stop the flesh slipping from their bones. Maybe this will take away my appetite, I think, as I put a single shrivelled leaf in my mouth. It tastes so bitter that I start to salivate.

Twenty-one

A knocking on the door. Three knocks, so soft that I wonder, am I dreaming? I am light-headed from hunger. It has been four days since the police raid and still no one has come.

'Hello?'

Knock knock knock. It is David. He has come to fetch me.

I crawl out of bed, creep to the door and sit down next to it.

'David? Is it you?'

No answer. Silence and then, again, knock knock knock.

Without thinking, I reply, knock knock knock.

A pause.

Knock knock. Louder this time. Clear, distinct.

I knock-knock back.

'David, is that you? Please, could you get someone to open the door? I haven't eaten for four days.'

Another pause.

One knock, so soft.

'David? David?'

Nothing.

~

Five and a half days. Still no sign of David. No Doctor Ongani, no George or Peter. I am so hungry that all I can do is lie on my bed all day, a blanket wrapped tightly around me like a mother's arms. Last night I ate the last of the toothpaste. Toothpaste doesn't take away hunger, but it tricks the mind into thinking that maybe it has eaten something. I do have water. That is fortunate. There is a sink in the corner of the room. Thirst is worse than hunger. But I can drink as much as I want. I have already tried drinking so as not to feel so hungry. It would be better if there was a stove that I could heat it on, I think to myself. I would need a pot too. Hot water fills the belly better than cold.

But I have no stove and no pot, and so I have to drink the water cold, directly from the tap. It only makes my stomach gurgle.

It is fortunate that I am not thirsty, I tell myself, pulling the blanket tighter. I have heard it said that a person can last three weeks without food but only three or four days without water. David. Did David tell me that? He will not abandon me, I tell myself, closing my eyes. Try to sleep. You are so tired. Soon David will come. He will unlock the door, pick you up in his arms and you two will be free.

The door opens and three men enter. I know their faces, have seen them before, but at first I cannot remember their names. But they know me. They step in and close the door behind them. One stands at the door to guard it. I think that they are expecting me to put up a fight. *Fight, Chipo.* Mama's voice in my mind. I close my eyes. No. I think no, as Julius and his friend rush forward.

Epilogue

THE PRESENT

The day is well on its way. I can see all the activity down below. The cars. The pigeons. The people. I can see what haunts them and I can see who will live, thrive and who will soon be swallowed by this city and die.

Gone sounds like shone. I never shone, but now that I am gone I can do as I wish. I start each day by putting myself back together. Dead hand, dead heart, dead leg, dead head. From head to foot I make the puzzle of me fit, and that which in life I found ugly I now find beautiful.

Alone. Lone. Lonely. I am never lonely. Apart from my memories, I have my own ghosts for company. My brother. Sometimes I visit him in the small hours, when he is lying awake on his crumpled blanket, his latest girlfriend sleeping beside him. He cannot see me, but he can feel me, and then my Coca-Cola-brown brother goes pale, as pale as I am, and it is good, for that moment, to be close to him again.

And not only him. If I want, I can visit the stadium too, where that last soccer game was played. The famous final. I am the now still grass and the ants marching determinedly over the sand, beneath that grass. I am the empty stands and the sweat and stains in the players' changing rooms. And I am the memories of hope and of loss, of victory and of despair, which lingered there, like damp morning mist, not so long ago. I travel further. Leave Johannesburg's blushing, bruised skyline. Over its crackling electric fences and yawning security guards, until I find Jean-Paul. I want to tell him that I am sorry. Meanwhile, on the other side of the country, David and Peter sit at a corner table. All around them carefree revellers laugh, joke. But the brothers do not hear. Peter's bottle of beer is warm, still untouched. And David? My darling David now drinks like a fish.

I fly further. Cross borders. Go back to Beitbridge. At least once a week I hover over the spot where our house and Mama's Old Trafford once stood. Sadness calls me down, even though I know that Mama is gone, our old house too, and our dreams, well, they were long ago pounded as fine as sadza *dust.*

I look. I watch. Then once again it is time for me to move on.

Acknowledgements

Thank you: Thomas, Leaticia, Jessie, Donald, Tembi, Guy, Paul, the Jean-Pierres, Alice, Jerome, Papi, Blessing, Tariro and all the others, who shared their stories with me about leaving home and crossing the African continent in the hopes of a better life.

Thank you, Nwabisa, for your openness and trust. Thank you, Ben-Carl, for the title. Thank you, Professor Duncan Brown and the UWC Arts Faculty, for your generous support. Thank you to Graham Mort, for being a superb supervisor and insightful reader. Thank you, Antjie, for your perceptive advice. Thank you, Tembi Charles, for spotting the 'lies'. Thank you, Alfred, for your diligence. Thank you, Fourie and Fanie, for being pleasures to work with.